The Gradual Elephant

Tembo Mpole

H. S. Toshack

Illustrations by Nelson McAlister

Other books in the series:

Paka Mdogo
The Meerkat Wars

First published in Great Britain
by
PakaMdogo Press 2010

A CIP record of this book is available from the British Library

ISBN 978-0-9563236-1-3

A set of free teaching resources (structured in line with the UK National Literacy Strategies but designed to help all 7-12 year old readers explore the text fully, and extend their enjoyment of it) is available in the *Paka Mdogo* section of the LitWorks.com website. Go to http://www.litworks.com/childrens.php.

Baragandiri National Park is just as large as it was the first time Sheena, a little black-and-white cat, came here for adventures (and had more of them than she bargained for).

This time she promises to be more careful; but she's not very good at keeping her promises.

The Baragandiri Map on Pages 6 and 7 will show you how big the Park is, and help you to follow Sheena's travels with Mpole, the Gradual Elephant, as he tries to pass **Mitihani Saba** - The Seven Tests.

Sheena will face some tests of her own before her second trip to Baragandiri is over...

To Africa...
...and with many thanks to Janet again

Contents

Chapter One: Safari Nyingine

'Bang!'

The first door.

'Crash!'

The second door.

Dad Allen had slammed the rear doors of the Land Rover shut. The sound was just the same as it had been at the beginning of the first journey Sheena had made to Baragandiri, where life was amazing.

She was just as well hidden now as she had been on that occasion six months ago: this time she had sneaked into a little space behind the rear seat on which Amy and Thomas were already curled up, surrounded by the things they thought would help them survive the bumpy eight-hour drive – four pillows, six packets of sweets, Annie the Favourite Doll (Amy's), Izzy the Favourite I-Pod (Thomas's), a boxing glove (Thomas had threatened to punch Annie if Amy annoyed him), a pair of scissors (Amy had threatened to snip Thomas's earphones if he punched Amy), and some plastic bags for being sick into. They remembered the first journey to Baragandiri well.

Sheena had brought along only her excitement.

'Safari Njema! – Safe Journey!' The askari's farewell was the same, too, as the campus gate squealed and clanged open and the Land Rover swung out into the road.

Sheena was going North again.

TZL
8046

Chapter Two: Swila

You may know some of this already:

- Sheena was a little black-and-white cat with a stumpy tail.
- She lived with the Allen family – Dad and Mum Allen (teachers at an international school in Africa) and Amy and Thomas (very high-spirited children she was very fond of).
- She had stowed away in the family Land Rover the last time the Allens went on a camping safari to Baragandiri National Park.
- She had got lost, had adventures, saved Amy and Thomas from being eaten by a very old but very dangerous lioness, and decided that she probably wouldn't want to go on safari ever again...

Yet here she was, squeezed back into the tight gap between a tent bag and a large cardboard box that smelled of biscuits – the kind Amy and Thomas liked, not her cat biscuits.

There were no cat biscuits on board since there was no cat as far as the Allens knew. They'd have been startled to find her there; and they'd have been startled enormously to learn even a bit of what she had got up to last time. They hadn't known she had travelled with them, and by a piece of catmagic (same as catcleverness, really) she had arranged to be lying on the sofa by the time Amy and Thomas rushed into the house to squeeze her and make up for having left her behind (even though they hadn't).

So why *had* she Done It Again?

Because of the smells. The smell of hot grass like new-baked bread. The smells that told stories; the smells that gave warnings; the smells of animals who were wholly alive (not like sleepy Safi the campus dog, and the other cats who lived nearby and thought about nothing more exciting than the next bowl of cat biscuits). She had never managed to get those smells completely out of her nostrils.

After she had been home for a little while, that last time, she had woken up one morning to realise that she had never *fully* woken up since she returned. She was living in a weak version of the trance she had gone into to make the Land Rover journeys, both North and back home, less uncomfortable. Life was just too easy; and it would be too easy to live it like this for as many years as she could see ahead of her. She wasn't a young cat, and before she was old she wanted to smell many more smells, even if some of them frightened her half to death.

So there and then she had said: 'Next time they go, I go!'

Here she was, then, jammed in this tight space which she immediately made bigger and more comfortable by slipping into another traveltrance.

Then they were there.

'There' was the Baragandiri Park Gate, where the Allens had to sign in and pay the necessary charges. Sheena, now wide awake, stayed absolutely still in her hiding place while that was happening. She had a clearer idea this time around what the list of park fees might include:

'Fees for Tourists – '
'Fees for Residents – '
'Fees for Citizens – '

'Fees for Vehicles – '.

It would not say:

'Fees for Household Pets – '.

In fact it might say:

'Fees for Locking Up Household Pets
Who Shouldn't Have Come Here
in the
First Place – '.

The Land Rover tipped slightly to one side as Dad Allen climbed back in. Sheena knew a bit about Land Rovers, since she had listened often enough to teachers who worked at the Allens' school discussing the Fun and Folly of Owning an old Land Rover. A Land Rover was something you had to have if you lived in Africa, and you spent a lot of time wishing you didn't have it. The Allen Family called theirs *Great White*; and Dad Allen seemed to be perpetually afraid that he was about to be bitten by it, in the area of the pocket. It had tipped to one side now because the front shock absorbers had gone. ('Gone' was a mechanics' term for 'might as well not be there'.)

The rear springs had 'gone', too, which is one reason why Sheena wanted to hear that they wouldn't be driving much further: her own rear springs had suffered quite enough for one day.

'Tembo Campsite.' That was Dad Allen's news.

'On the banks of the Ubi River. Not far. We just need to cross the Main Bridge, turn left, drive down past the Lodge and cross a couple of fords.' That was Dad Allen's *good* news – for them all, since for the last two hours the haze of Sheena's trance had been penetrated by sharp grumblings from Amy and Thomas, and both the boxing glove and the scissors had been waved threateningly in the air, several times.

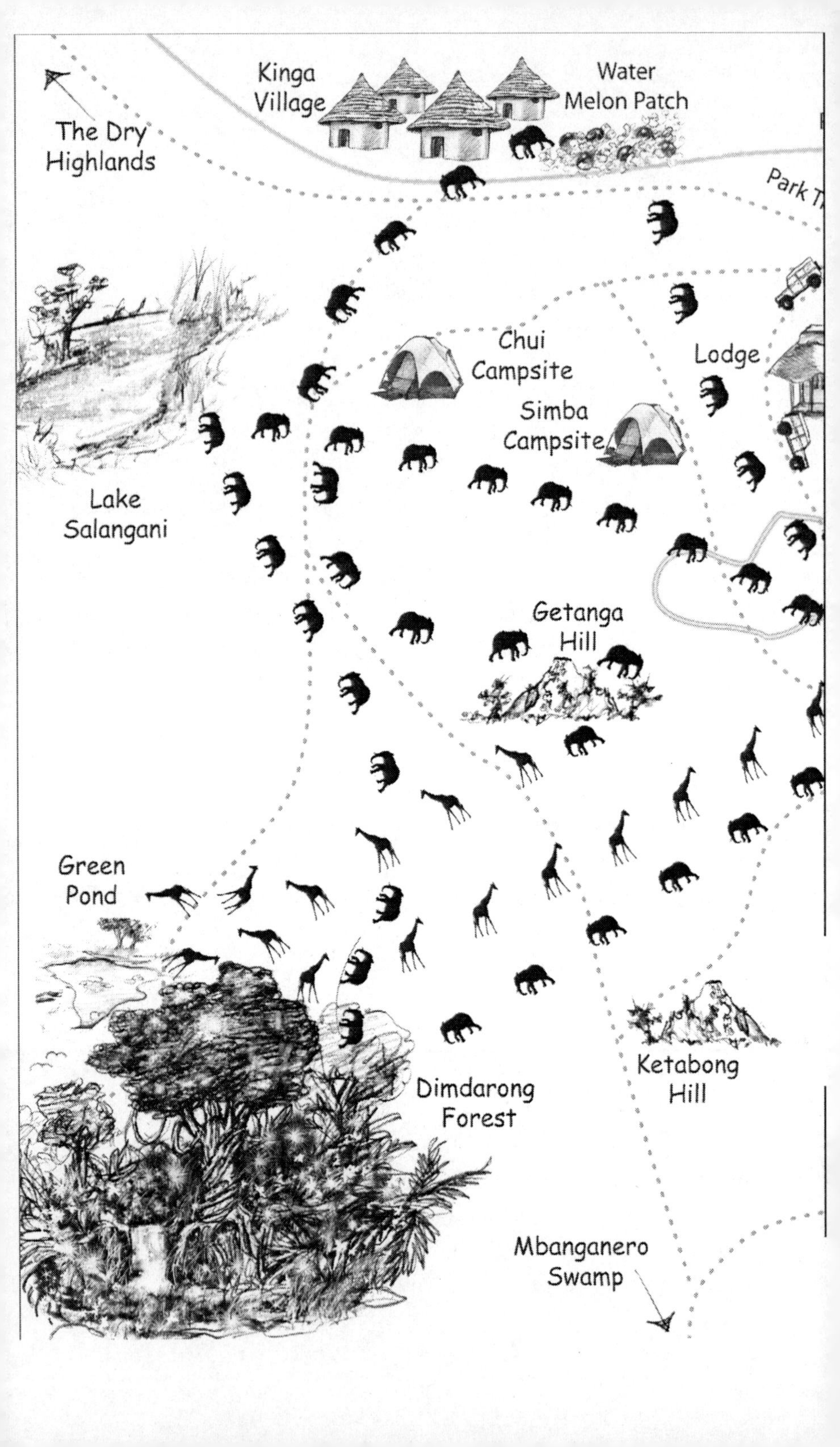

Kinga Village
Water Melon Patch
The Dry Highlands
Park Tr
Chui Campsite
Lodge
Simba Campsite
Lake Salangani
Getanga Hill
Green Pond
Ketabong Hill
Dimdarong Forest
Mbanganero Swamp

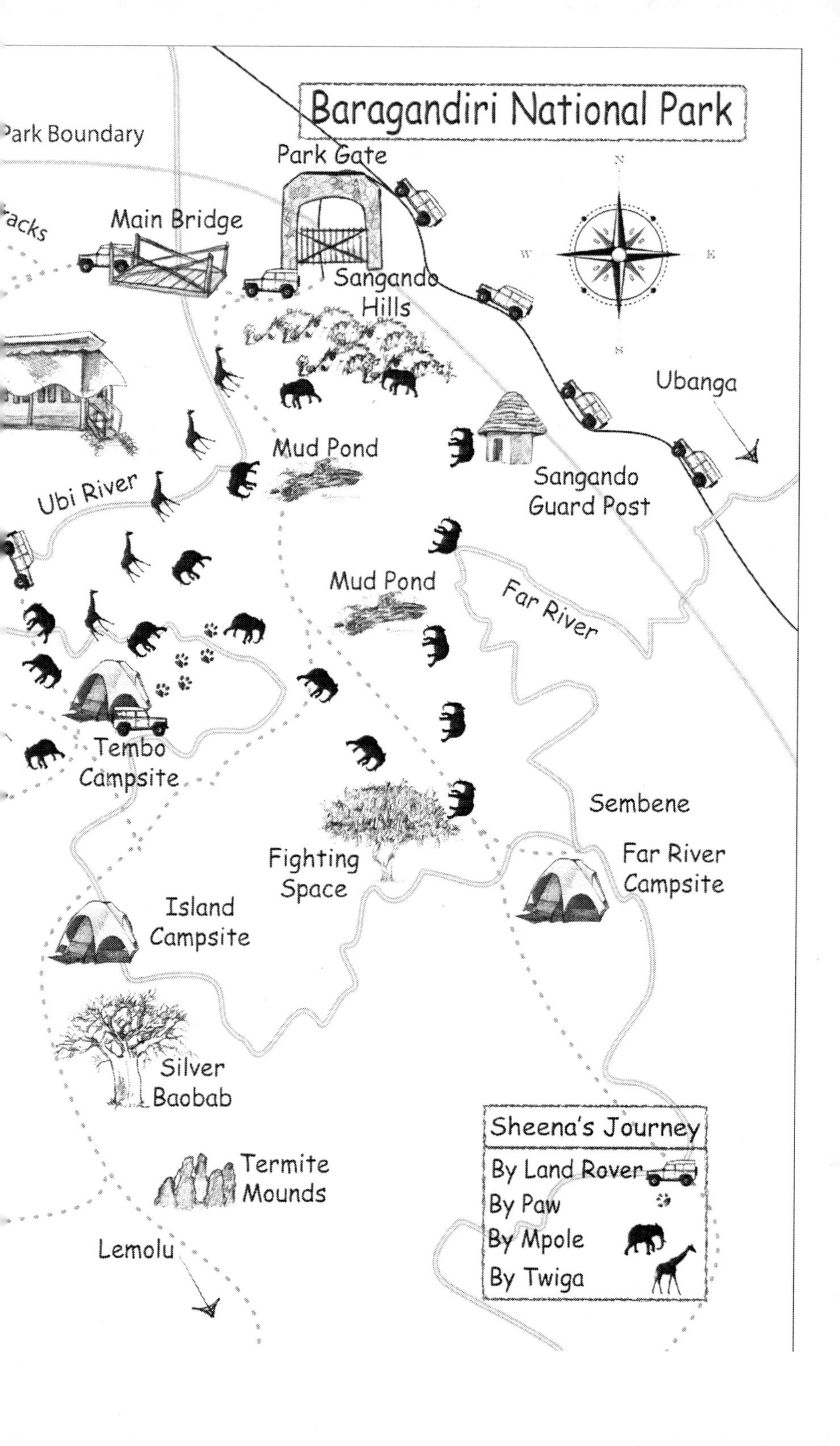

Baragandiri National Park
Park Boundary
Park Gate
Main Bridge
Sangando Hills
Mud Pond
Ubi River
Sangando Guard Post
Ubanga
Mud Pond
Far River
Tembo Campsite
Sembene
Fighting Space
Far River Campsite
Island Campsite
Silver Baobab
Termite Mounds
Lemolu
Sheena's Journey
By Land Rover
By Paw
By Mpole
By Twiga

It was all good news for Sheena for another reason. She knew what 'tembo' meant in Kiswahili. 'Elephant.'

There were several things she nearly regretted about her last visit here, when she had had to run around the Park looking for *Great White* and its occupants, all of which she had foolishly lost. She nearly regretted them in the sense that they had nearly happened to her, and if they had she would have regretted them very much indeed. What things? Oh, being swallicked by a jackal (*swallicked* = swallowed, sicked up and swallowed again), strangulped by a python, and so on.

The one thing she did actually regret, however, was not seeing an elephant. (In truth, she *had* seen one, but it was a long, long way away, and she glimpsed it only briefly from an eagle's nest where she was in imminent danger of being re-organised as a snack – so that didn't count.) More than seeing one: being close to, hearing, smelling of course, even talking to it if she was lucky. While she was in Baragandiri that previous time, she had come to realise just how much living things can learn from each other, no matter how unpromising (or downright dangerous) the circumstances.

Elephants have such a reputation for being wise; and they look so old even when they are young; and they are so big that everything they do, including speak, they do weightily. And cats are so Curious, as Sheena had often demonstrated. So of course she wanted to see (etc.) an elephant. Where better to do that than at Tembo Campsite?

When they got there she had to be very nippy. She needed to nip out of the back of the Land Rover after the doors were opened but before the unloading started: she didn't want to be unloaded, herself, into the stern gaze of the Allen parents, who would have felt the need to do Something Official about her.

Luckily, there were lots of distractions for the Allens – a debate about where to pitch the tents, a discussion as to whether those droppings over there were from a gazelle or something much more sinister, an argument between Amy and Thomas about who was the owner of the empty sweet packet, as opposed to the half-full one. Amy was more than half-fully opposed to the idea that *she* was.

In a black-and-white flash Sheena was out of the Land Rover, then behind a tree, then up the tree, all unseen. Lying comfortably along a leafy branch, shaded from the late afternoon sun, she could watch at leisure the setting-up of the Allen camp and all that went with it – the huffing and hauling, the humping and heaping, the hammering and hopping. (The hopping was when Dad Allen walloped his thumb instead of a tent peg. He said he would need to take an antidote to the pain, which might consist of driving back up to the Lodge, a little later, for Sundowners – whatever they were. Sheena suspected he might actually be feeling the need for an antidote to the hard work.)

Through it all she was not just watching, she was watching *over*. Only she knew how close the last family safari had come to tragedy. She had been nearly eaten herself, more than once; much worse, however, she had nearly lost Amy and Thomas to Nyanya, a raggedy old lion with worn teeth but a sharp eye for an easy meal. Nothing like that must happen this time. She would stay around the camp-site and keep a look-out – from above, from below (in the long grass at the edge of the clearing), from the sky if necessary, even if she had to flatter another eagle into using her as ballast in an acrobatic aerial extravaganza.

If she wanted to have adventures, it would have to be in between times. Amy and Thomas's safety must come first. That was what she told herself, and she believed it so firmly that it amounted to a promise.

In between what times, though? In between the time when Thomas and Amy crawled into the tent and then their sleeping bags, and the time next morning when they crawled out again? Surely it was at night that they would be most at risk from toothy wild animals?

Sheena was fast realising that this was a full-time task she had set herself. 'The jungle never sleeps' (where had she heard that?) and neither could she; nor could she go off on jaunts of her own…

…Not very far, at least. Already she felt a wor coming on, and feared it would soon turn into a moi, and even a boap.

Wors and mois were a troublesome part of her life. Everybody (every animal with a thinking brain that is, and that's most animals and most people) experienced them; but Sheena found them particularly difficult. Worst of all was when they turned into full-blown boaps.

She had tried to explain all three, once, to her Caribbean tabby-cat friend Toby. She had discovered a mouse nest under the patio of the apartment where she lived with the Allens (Toby lived in the apartment above). That should have been a source of great delight and an opportunity for much crunching of little bones; but when she nosed her way into the nest the baby mice, alone there, were so helpless – pink, shiny and struggling things with closed eyes and lolling heads – that she had just backed out and left them.

'Couldn't do it,' she said to Toby. 'Won't do it. Promise not to.' (She wasn't sure who she was making the promise to.) 'Do without.'

Later in the day she had found herself back at the nest. She had had a wor. A wor was a weakening of resolution. She had resolved to stay away, but here she was.

'I'll just see how they are,' she said to herself. Before she realised it, one of the tiny wriggling things was in her jaws. She had had a moi – a modification of intention. (The big words she used to explain what was happening were just like fancy packaging, designed to hide the fact that what was in the box was really very simple.)

Before she walked slowly back to where Toby was lying in the shade of a tree she had committed a complete boap – breaking of a promise. She felt bad (except in the stomach).

'Don't feel bad,' was all Toby said when she told him what she'd done; but he couldn't explain why she shouldn't.

'Down a bit,' was what he said next (she was licking him at the time); and that was the end of that discussion about the importance of doing what you said you would do, and not doing what you said you wouldn't.

Her wor now was brought on by the faint sound of something moving among the trees a little way along the dry river bed next to which the Allens had pitched their tents. What was it? Something interesting, no doubt: everything was interesting, here. She had to know.

'I'll just go a little way, and stay within sight of the Land Rover.'

The Allens were busy making a fire, which involved more huffing, this time at ground level: all Sheena could see was a circle of khaki-covered behinds with a little plume of smoke drifting up from the centre. The family were safe for the moment, unless they were *much* too successful with the fire. In any case they might well be driving off soon, for those Sundowner things, and she wouldn't easily be able to go with them. So she jumped down from the branch on the side of tree away from the tents, and trotted off briskly.

'Soon be back!' she said, to the tree as much as to anyone else.

She wasn't back soon. First of all she had a moi, caused by the fact that the small sound she had heard nearby was actually a large sound further away. She therefore had to run on quite a distance past the big tree she'd intended to stop at. Then there was a further moi, which led to a total boap; but you may decide they weren't altogether her fault, when you hear what happened.

She had stayed close to the sandy river bed, and had wound her way in and out of a series of low, pale-green trees standing in short, springy grass. She was quickly beyond the large tree and out of sight of the Land Rover; but there was no danger that she would get lost, since the river bed would lead her back again. The rustling in the trees was further on, past that bush.

Also past that bush there was a snake, curled up in a patch of long grass that she was just about to run through. It was like a half-hidden coil of stripey brown rope, and if she had continued running she might well have got it wrapped around her legs. As she rounded the bush, however, the rope reared up from the grass and became an angry reptile hanging in the air over her and swaying, as if it was suspended on an invisible string.

At the same time she too had reared up, backwards, in surprise (but also in readiness: her claws had come out automatically). Her defensive instincts had pulled her upright, as if *she* had had her string yanked from above. She couldn't stay like that for long, however, and almost immediately dropped back onto all fours.

The snake's eyes glittered on either side of its pointed head: as it swayed, left then right and back again, Sheena could see each eye in turn, and they were like signal lamps flashing a dark message without giving out any real light. The scales on its head were light brown with black edges. Its pink throat was wide and flat, as if it had been run over by a car: there were even black stripes across it, like tyre-marks; but Sheena had seen pictures of such snakes before, in Thomas's wildlife books, and knew that this was a cobra, and that its flat neck was called a hood.

The last time Sheena had met a snake it had cheated by falling on her from a great height and crushing her with its great weight. This one was at least behaving like a normal snake. It had a hood, but its *eyes* were not hooded: it was doing nothing to hide its fierceness.

Sheena knew that also unlike Chatu the python this snake was poisonous. Its fangs were all too obvious when it opened its mouth – large and yellowish-white, curving down from its upper jaw and looking very sharp indeed.

Fortunately she had come to a sudden halt about five feet

short of the snake, beyond its striking range. It was itself hardly more than five feet long, and if it lunged all the way towards her it would fall flat on its very sharp indeed fangs. (Sheena was ready to look very sharp indeed in her own way, and spring backwards.)

Cats can also be very Casual. When she was in Baragandiri before, Sheena had demonstrated a whole string of the C-words cats are, and on that trip Casual was something she had had lots of occasion to be. Casual is sometimes the best thing *to* be when you're faced with danger.

'Oh hullo snake,' Sheena said.

'Ssss,' said the snake, softly, through thin lips which, Sheena now saw, had edges that were black like the edges of its scales. The snake's cold, hard stare unsettled her, and she decided to try and turn its attention to something else.

'Any idea what that noise is, over there?' she asked. The loud rustling and shaking among the trees further along the river bed had started up again.

'Over there' did not cause the snake to turn its head one bit.

'I'm more interessted in what'ss happening over here,' said the reptile, still hissily.

It was clearly trying to make up its mind about Sheena.

Sheena had always thought of herself as a little animal with big potential. The snake seemed to think the same; but was it a potential to provide a big meal or to be a big pain in the grass – in other words Trouble?

'I'm sorry. Would you mind wery much if I circumwented you, I mean vent around you? Not that I vant to cause you any inconwenience.'

Sheena's memories of her awful experience with Chatu had made her nervous, and she tried to hide it by being polite and using long words. Her jitteriness was poking through her politeness, however, and showed itself in her verbal wobbles (which she would probably have pronounced werbal vobbles). The snake's fangs were very large, and snakes can move very quickly. This one was well big enough to kill her with one strike, and her death would be very painful. The snake would then probably unhinge its lower jaw and swallow her down slow and whole, lumpy and furry though she was.

That might have been what was in the snake's mind too: but this strange black-and-white creature would be a very big mouthful for a snake which although long was quite slender. If it couldn't eat it there wasn't much point in killing it: that would be a waste of venom, and you never knew when you'd need a quick squirt of fang-fluid.

Maybe it wasn't as fat as it looked, though, maybe under its fur it was a skinny thing which would slip down a long throat quite easily. The snake hadn't eaten for ages: it could go a whole year without food, but the year was almost up. It had been deceived before by a scrawny animal which had looked much plumper than it was – animals had a habit, when in danger, of fluffing themselves up to look big and fierce. How much did this one weigh? Being a clever sort of snake, it liked to deliver just enough venom to paralyse its prey: 'Take care of your droplets, and your drops will take of themselves' was a part of its snake lore.

If it didn't manage to paralyse this creature quickly, what might happen? Anything, was the answer. This was after all the jungle, and 'The jungle's full of leaps' (that was the snake-lore version of the little proverb Sheena had remembered from somewhere): this animal looked a bit too much like a serval cat, in spite of its black-and-white patches; and servals had been known to jump on snakes when they least expected it, and bite them where they could least do anything about it – behind the head.

Just thinking about that made the snake tower up higher, and Sheena responded by standing up on her back legs again, claws pointing forward (although they were a poor match for the pair of daggers glistening at the front of the snake's mouth, with traces of a yellowish fluid at their tips. This was obviously a front-fanged snake; and Sheena was afraid that its brain might be front-fanged also – inclined to strike first and think afterwards.)

The rear-off couldn't continue indefinitely, however. Sheena couldn't keep her balance, for one thing, and dropped forward onto all fours once more. The snake subsided a little, and so did the danger of a mutually-destructive launch.

'What's your name, by the way?' she asked. 'The only other snake I've met was called Chatu.'

'Chatu? Chatu? Ssstupid python? Great lump of writhing flesh: just one big mussscle! No brain. No venom. No delicasssy of movement. No finesssse.

'No, I'm not a chatu. I'm a ssswila' (another stretched word – with a touch of pride in the way it was uttered).

Sheena guessed 'swila' meant 'cobra'. Cobras were famed for the subtlety of their movement, the power of their poison, and their bad temper. Chatu on the other hand had been clumsy, poison-less and quite calm about his first (and unsatisfactory) encounter with a house-cat.

This snake was not calm. It obviously did not trust Sheena (why should it?), either not to attack or not to run away suddenly. It continued to sway in front of her, as if trying to locate a spot on her body to aim for in a swift forward lunge. Sheena found herself moving to the same sideways rhythm, left, right, left, right, as if the snake's black eyes were polished jet beads on a gold chain, being swung rhythmically before her gaze by a tall, slim hypnotist, so that she was forced to follow their movement with her whole body. 'Gaze' was fast becoming 'glaze': she felt a sssleepiness washing over her. The brighter the snake's eyes became, the duller and heavier Sheena's felt to be. She knew she must not succumb, must not sink: that would allow the snake to slither within striking distance, rise again and . . . and then she was lost.

So she began to move backwards, slowly. That's not an easy thing for cats to do: they usually only move forward. The best Sheena could manage now (she didn't want the snake to notice) was a careful wiggle of her back paws, first one and then the other, into the grass behind her. That had the effect of elongating her body. A quiet little thrust of her front paws shortened her again so that she ended up a fraction further away from the snake. Then she repeated her rear-paw wiggle, and her front-paw thrust, so that she inched gradually back from the danger zone, like a very large, slow caterpillar in reverse.

All the while she tried to keep up a patter of talk, partly to cover her movement, partly to resist the sleepiness flooding out towards her from the snake's bright eyes. She rambled on about things that she thought might interest a snake, making up most of the details – details about the shortage of mice (she knew snakes loved mice); the rampages of mongooses (she also knew snakes hated mongooses – 'Or is it mongeese?' she asked the snake by way of a further distraction); the comparative merits of old termite mounds and hollow tree-trunks as places to live. There was a large termite-mound a few feet away from where the snake was lying, with a hole at its base. Was that the snake's home? If so, it would live there alone: there was no such thing as a snake family. No wonder then if this swila was bad-tempered: that was an inhospitable-looking place to have to crawl into when you wanted to rest. She'd slept in a termite mound, once (and very well too), but wouldn't have wanted to call it home.

So Sheena's thoughts rambled, like her talk, as she worked her body slowly backwards. All the while the snake swayed; and all the while it knew what Sheena was up to; and all the slow while it was making up its mind that yes, this little animal would probably provide a good meal after all, so it shouldn't be allowed to shuffle any further away. Just when Sheena thought she was far enough out of range of the snake's strike to turn and make a dash for it, the snake struck.

How could it? It was only five feet long, and by now Sheena was six feet away.

Sheena had made a mistake. 'Swila' didn't just mean 'cobra'; it meant 'spitting cobra'. This one spat.

Sheena saw it spit, so clearly. It was the last thing she saw. It was as if she was watching the whole event on a wildlife programme back home with the Allens: the camera suddenly slowed, and its focus sharpened, so that she could see droplets of yellow venom form in the tiny black holes at the front of the snake's fangs. Then the venom flew towards her, in a stream and with a long hiss. For an instant she had a picture in her mind of Thomas doing something like that, squirting soda out at Amy through his front teeth. Then the poison was in her eyes and she was blind. The tv screen had gone blank and dark, her world had gone blank and dark. Some of the poison ran down her face and onto her nose. It smelt sharp and bitter. She sneezed.

She was painfully blind. Burningly blind. She felt as if her eyeballs were dissolving in acid, being melted down to a hot liquid which would run out of her eye sockets and leave them pitifully empty.

That would not kill her; but the snake now could. All it had to do was slither close and sink its fangs into her, injecting poison, the same poison, into her body. She had jumped back violently when she felt the pain in her eyes, but had become snagged in the bush behind her; and now she did not know which way to struggle, imagined the snake sliding towards her, could not think because of the agony, could hardly move because of the branches among which she was caught. It would only be a matter of time before she felt two sharp stab-wounds (where – in her shoulder, or her neck?) and then the pumping of the venom into her veins and the quick paralysis and the slow swallowing into darkness, the most horrible part of what would be a horrible death.

Through her pain she heard the snake moving towards her, making a lot of noise. Too much noise, surely? That was not snake-slither, it was animal-crash. It was like, but louder than, the sound she had heard among the river-bank trees, the sound that had brought her here. It was close, closer, and the ground shook and she feared that she was about to be trampled, not stabbed after all.

There was a final trembling of the ground as if a heavy vehicle was passing (but there was no sound of an engine) then a silence. Then a noise half-way between a sniff and a whoosh, very close to her so that she jumped again, and started to struggle among the branches – still hurting horribly in the eyes but a bit less frightened in the mind. The sound had not been aggressive, more enquiring.

Then there was an enquiring voice also, a strong voice trying not to be loud.

'How are you, little cat? Do your eyes hurt? Don't worry, nothing bad is going to happen to you now.'

Sheena was still struggling with the bush and with her pain. The branches were beginning to let go of her, but the pain would not.

'Here, let me help you.'

Sheena felt the springy branch above her, which had held her down, being lifted, and she half rolled, half jumped free. Then stopped. It was too much. Moving was too much when she could see nothing, it was too dangerous. Maybe the snake was still in front of her. The pain, also, was too much. She licked a paw vigorously, then rubbed it over her eyes. It made no difference. Her eyeballs were still dissolving in agony. She did not have enough saliva to wash them clear: the encounter with the snake had been totally mouth-drying.

Then there was another 'sniff-whoosh', this time close behind her, and she automatically jumped forward and away from the sound, blind as she was. The jarring as she landed made her swollen eyeballs feel like they were going to burst out of her head altogether. They were hurting so badly, as if they were being gnawed at by a small animal with sharp teeth, that she considered scratching them out herself just to be rid of the pain.

'Sorry – I didn't mean to startle you,' said the voice, and it really did sound apologetic.

Sheena had landed on something tangled, which wrapped itself around her legs as she tried to scrabble away.

'The snake! The snake!' She could imagine the fangs sinking into her leg.

'Yes, the snake – but in a new flat version,' said the voice.

Sheena stopped scrabbling with her paws and used them to feel instead. It was indeed the snake, but it was not moving. She could feel its scales, but they no longer sheathed a firm, cylindrical body. This was like standing on a garden hose that had gone flat. Sheena knew, because one way she used to annoy Dad Allen was by standing on his hose when he was trying to wash *Great White*. If only she was back in the garden at home now!

There would be no pain there.

'It was just about to bite you. I don't like snakes.'

Sheena thought she would probably feel grateful, soon, to whoever or whatever had rescued her; but for the moment she only felt the fire in her eyes. She tried washing them again, with no effect.

'Wait, wait, I can help.'

Sheena was aware of something moving over her body, then curling round underneath it. It felt like another snake, but a very big and heavy one, more like Chatu the python, and she tensed herself to jump again, blindly and no matter where. Having escaped being stabbed, then being trampled, she was in no mind to be squeezed to death instead.

She *was* squeezed, but gently; and she was lifted off the ground so that she couldn't have jumped anyway. Then she was carried, in a sickening, swaying motion that was made worse by the fact that she could see nothing, even when she forced her eyes open against the pain. She soon felt ill.

'I feel sick. Please put me down.'

She was slowly lowered to the ground.

'Where are you taking me? Who are you? How can you help me? Ow my eyes! Will I ever see again?'

'I'm not taking you far. Just to the river bed. Wait till we get there and all your other questions will be answered. Let's try to move again – unless you'd care to walk?'

Walking would be too difficult, Sheena decided. Cats are usually extremely careful about where they put their feet, and she couldn't bring herself to take even one step forward in this awful darkness. She allowed herself to be picked up once more. She was swung from side to side as they moved forward, and she soon felt sick again. Then, however, she was placed carefully on what felt like sandy ground.

'Wait there a moment.'

A soft thumping began. The ground shook at each thump. It sounded like Dad Allen hammering in the tent pegs with his large wooden mallet (before he hit his thumb).

She made herself open her eyes again, first one, then the other. She still couldn't see out of either of them. There was just a red, painful light. The air itself made them sting badly, so she shut them again.

The thumping noise grew gradually more muffled, and now there was a scraping noise as well, and a pattering between thumps as if sand were being scattered. This was digging, surely. But digging why? (Graves came to mind, but Sheena didn't want to think about them.)

Eventually she could hear a new noise, a small splashing that followed each thump, as if lumps of sand were falling into water. Suddenly there was a big slurp, and a moment later and from the darkness above her came a solid deluge of cool water, 'Whoosh!', which almost forced her down onto her stomach by its sheer weight. She was thoroughly drenched. She gasped. There was a pause while the water ran off her.

'Try to open your eyes next time.'

She forced her eyes open, although she cringed at the thought of anything going in them which might make them hurt more.

Slurp…Whoosh!

More water, cascading heavily over her head as if from a bucket. This time it washed into her open eyes as well, and she immediately felt a lessening of the pain.

'More please! More!'

She got more, several times, until she was shivering. She had managed to suck in some of the water running over her face, and that had helped quench her thirst.

The pain in her eyes had almost gone. What was left was only an ache; but there was still a darkness where there should have been light, a greyness where there should have been colour, a smooth, still wall where there should have been shapes and movement.

'I still can't see!'

'You will, little cat, you will.'

Then she felt herself being picked up once more and carried back to where the grass was long and soft and brushed past her on either side, then laid carefully down. All she wanted to do was stay there and rest. She felt suddenly weak. Had some of the poison got into her nose in spite of her sneeze? Was she going to die after all?

She passed into unconsciousness.

She woke up once. The darkness was even deeper (was it night-time?) but there were lighter patches in it, and colourless shapes. She seemed to be in a building of some sort: there were four thick pillars around her, and a roof above which swayed slightly.

Then there was only darkness once more.

Chapter Three: Mitihani Saba

The early sun woke her. She felt its warmth on her face. She could also see its light, through her eyelids: the world was a much brighter place now than it had been when she fell asleep.

Had she fallen asleep or apoison? Had some of the snake's venom got into her system, perhaps up her nostrils, perhaps through a scratch on her face from the bush back into which she had jumped? She had slept very deeply, and now felt weak and shaky.

Why couldn't she open her eyes? There was a world out there to see, if only she could get her eyelids apart; but they were glued together.

Then the ground shook a little, and something came between her and the sun's warmth.

'Oh, I see. Your eyelids are stuck. Good job I brought some water. I thought you might need another shower.'

Sheena braced herself. *Whoosh!* She was wet again. It seemed this shower tap was either on or off, with nothing in between; and when it was on it was very on.

She rubbed her eyes hard with her front paws and felt her eyelids loosen. There was still some stickiness between the lids, but she forced them open one side at a time.

Yes, the world was brighter, almost too bright; but it was blurred, as if she was looking out through a rainy window…at something very large, and grey – not grey because she was still half-blind, but grey because it was grey. There in front of her, against the sharp blue of the sky, was the unmistakable shape of an elephant, with a golden glow around its edges.

Slowly her eyes cleared, and her sight sharpened…and she had something of a surprise.

Her next feeling, strangely, was one of disappointment. The animal that had helped her last night had seemed so big, and powerful. This one was only a few feet tall, six at most. Could it be the same creature?

'Er, thank you, thank you very much. You and your big friend have been very kind. I can see now – a bit vaguely, but seeing's relieving.'

'My big friend? There's only me. I don't have any big friends, actually. And I know *I'm* not big.

'I understand why you've made the mistake, though. When your eyes are shut, sounds always seem louder, and when you can't see something and have to imagine it, you can easily think it's larger than it really is. That's why you didn't realise I'm quite a small elephant.'

'I didn't realise you were an elephant at all,' Sheena began to say, but the elephant continued as if he hadn't heard her.

'But I will get bigger gradually. I'll be really big one day, you'll see!'

That was a rather strange thing for the elephant to say, and it was said with a touch of defiance, as if somebody had recently told him something different.

'Don't worry! You're quite big enough for me! Or rather, you were quite big enough to help me yesterday. Now I need to go,' Sheena said.

Then she fell over. Her legs just gave way beneath her and she found herself lying on the ground, feeling helpless.

'Oh dear, you aren't better yet. That sometimes happens with snakes – their poison begins to work again long after you think everything's fine.

'Swilas are worse than most snakes; and that was a banded swila – they're worse than most other swilas.'

('So they should be banned as well as banded,' Sheena thought to herself.)

'Swilas can kill a young elephant. That's why we trample them whenever they come close. A few years ago my baby brother Ombi went snuffling into a hole with his trunk, and when he pulled it out there was a swila hanging on the end. It had bitten him. He squealed and squealed, and whipped it around, but it wouldn't let go. My mother made him lower his trunk so that the swila was lying on the ground, and she walked on it from the tail forward until it opened its fangs and Ombi was able to pull his trunk away from it.

'He was sick for weeks – and that wasn't a very big snake, about half the size of yours.'

'Yours'? *Her* snake? She didn't want to own a snake, dead or alive (this one must surely be dead, from what she remembered of its flat feel under her paws). She knew, however, that the snake was now a part of her remembered life, and of her near-death which she would also remember so clearly. It was as if the snake, after it had been killed, had slithered into her mind and would always live somewhere inside it. It would come out in her dreams, she knew, every now and again, and she would be terrified until she had woken and knew that the world was still there (and that she was able to see it) and that the snake wasn't.

'You'd better stay here a while, until you're fully recovered. Or is there somewhere you'd rather I carried you?'

Sheena didn't fancy another carry. Truth to tell, she just wanted to lie where she was. The trees above her were beginning to provide some shade as the sun moved up into them; and her head ached. The thought of even the short, swaying distance the elephant had taken her the night before made her feel sick again.

Dad Allen, in a weak attempt to entertain the children on the long journey (and partly to take their minds off plastic bags) had begun telling old elephant jokes, most of them no better than Christmas cracker standard. One of the first, oldest and worst had been:

'How does an elephant travel when it wants to go a long way?'

'By trunk road.'

('What's a trunk road?' Amy had asked.)

Sheena had also, once, heard about a cat in America who had

travelled a thousand miles locked in the trunk of a car. As she listened to the story, she had imagined that being trapped in the swaying darkness would have surely made the cat feel sick. Travelling in the trunk of an elephant, wrapped in her own swaying darkness, had certainly had that effect on her.

'Thanks. I think I will just rest. Would it be possible to have some more water?'

She hadn't managed to catch much in her mouth when she was being decontaminated a few minutes earlier, and now she felt very thirsty again. Maybe there *was* some poison in her body, and the answer would be to dilute it by drinking lots.

'Back in a moment.'

Sheena watched the elephant walk off. He might not be very large, but when he moved he nevertheless did so ponderously: he placed his feet with care, and his heavy haunches rose and fell, rose and fell, as he went.

He didn't go far. By lifting her head (that hurt a bit: her joints all felt stiff) Sheena could see how short her journey of the night before had been. Just through the next stand of long grass the river bed, dry and sandy, stretched off to left and right. The elephant walked down into it and stopped near the middle. There was a hole in the sand. That must be the one he had dug. He inserted his trunk and there was a slurping noise once more. Then he turned and rocked steadily back to where Sheena lay, his trunk swinging heavily.

'Let's try this.'

The elephant's trunk was obviously full of water (some of it was dripping out of the end).

'Open your eyes, and your mouth.'

The elephant, who had said he was gradually growing bigger, must also be trying to do other things gradually, for the stream of water that now fell over Sheena's face had less force than the earlier ones, and she was able to gulp some down without spluttering too much. The water was cool, and fresh, and didn't taste at all leathery ('elephant trunky' had really been what she expected).

'Oh thank you!' (little gasp). 'That was very nice. Thank you for being gradual.'

'Have you had enough?'

'Yes.'

She watched as the elephant tipped his own head back, put the end of his trunk in his mouth, and let the remaining water gush down his throat. So that was how elephants drank! She'd imagined they simply sucked water up through their trunks as if through a straw, and that it then went straight down into their stomachs. This looked harder.

'It takes us a long time to learn how to do it, when we're very young,' the elephant explained, after she'd said why she was surprised. 'At the beginning, we can only stick our faces in the water and slurp it straight up into our mouths. Knowing how to use your trunk to drink is one sign that you're growing up.'

'How old are you, may I ask?'

Sheena's questions were one sign that *she* was *perking* up: she was becoming Curious again.

'Twelve. Almost grown-up.'

'That's not almost grown-up!' Sheena said, rather thoughtlessly. In cat terms it *was* grown-up (she herself was ten years old, and that was well on the way to being as grown-up as she was likely to get). She'd said it, however, because she had Thomas in mind. He was still a little boy in some ways, even though *he* was twelve. Her comment was thoughtless, and a bit unkind, mainly because this elephant seemed to feel that growing up, and growing big, were very important, and he obviously wanted to appear well on the way to being both big and up.

'My family thinks it is.'

There was a plaintive tone in the elephant's voice when he said that – a sad feeling as if something had passed that would not come again, and as if there was something not quite fair about that.

'I don't really feel almost grown-up; but now I have to be. I want to get older, of course, but not all at once. Now I have to do it suddenly.'

'I'll call you The Gradual Elephant if that will make you feel better; then you might feel it's ok to take things slowly.'

'Tembo Mpole': the elephant tried the new name, in Kiswahili, pronouncing the second part 'Umpolay'.

'I sort of like that. It fits, you see. Other elephants call me slow, but it's just that I like to think before I do things.

'I'd like time to think before I grow up any more. I'm not sure what I want to grow up into.'

'But you do want to grow up into an elephant, don't you?'

'Oh, yes, elephants are wonderful animals and I'm proud to be one.'

'And you do want to grow up into a male elephant?'

Sheena had taken a discreet look between the elephant's hind legs, and she *thought* she had asked the right question; but it was hard to tell. Elephants – young elephants at least – seemed to keep things well hidden, in that area. In any case she had listened to Mum and Dad Allen talking often enough, when Amy and Thomas weren't around, to know that such matters shouldn't be taken for granted, even if all the basic bits were in place.

'Yes, yes. Being a male is a lot more fun. But it's also more difficult, and that's something I need to think about. I'm not sure I can do it.'

'What do you mean, *do it*? Surely it just happens, unless you decide otherwise?'

'Not really. You have to Do It...Do Them, I mean.'

'Them?'

'Mitihani Saba. The Seven Tests.'

Sheena knew something about tests. There were always tests at the International School, and the family were always grumbling about them – Mum and Dad Allen because they had to set them, Amy and Thomas because they had to sit them. 'Set, sit – what a difference a vowel makes,' Sheena had said to herself when she was listening to both sides of the complaint banging against each other. 'There could be some fun in it, if every now and again the children got to set the tests and the teachers were made to sit them.'

Then there were the tests Amy and Thomas had to take because she was a Brownie and he was in the Boy Scouts. These seemed to be much more useful than the school tests, and involved collecting things, finding your way round in the countryside, spotting birds, cooking food (not birds, sadly) on a campfire, and looking after pets (Sheena had lived in luxury while Amy was taking her Pet Keeper test). The children got something to show for their efforts, too – bright badges to sew on their uniforms, a mite better than numbers or letters on a school report.

'Tell me,' Sheena asked.

'Young male elephants are allowed to stay with their families only until they're about my age. Then they start getting into trouble – fighting, refusing to do things, wandering off on their own. So they are Sent Out.'

'Sent Out?'

'Sent away, banished, made to live by themselves. They become Singletons.'

'Simpletons?'

'No!' The elephant was emphatic.

'*Singletons*. Single elephants, elephants who live by themselves.'

'That sounds a bit harsh. You mean live by themselves for

ever?'

Thomas was sometimes Sent Out – from the classroom, and once from the Allens' dining room when he had done something spectacular with his cabbage. But Sent Out for good? No, that couldn't happen.

'Well, they can live, on and off, with the other young males who have been Sent Out, and that's not too bad; but they can never again be part of a family. In fact they can never go *near* a family, not until they're old enough to mate properly. Then nobody can stop them coming into the herd to choose a female. They're too big by then, you see, and they get very bad-tempered.'

'Why are you Sent Out so soon?'

Sheena had without thinking included this elephant in the 'you'. He on the other hand had been using 'they', as if this didn't directly affect him, not yet. Whether or not he had realised what he was doing, he now switched to 'we', as if he had finally accepted that these things were happening to him, too.

'Because we cause trouble. Some of us think we're old enough to chase females, and that leads to fights with older males. We aren't allowed to be with females until we've proved we'd make good fathers. That's to make sure the herd stays strong.'

'What's a good father?'

Sheena was quite interested in that. There was sometimes discussion in the Allen household about whether or not Dad Allen was a good father. The discussion was usually started by Amy or Thomas when they weren't getting their own way; but Mum and Dad Allen occasionally talked about the same thing after the children had gone to bed. Underneath it all, despite the grumbles from Amy and Thomas, there seemed to be general and quiet agreement that he *was* good. That was the family's way (rather feeble, Sheena thought) of saying thank you.

The family next door, however, had a father who was not so good, and Sheena knew how much unhappiness that caused.

'Good' by elephant reckoning seemed much more straightforward, however.

'A strong and healthy one,' said the young elephant.

'That's all?'

That was rather like saying that a good human father was one with plenty of money. The elephant seemed puzzled at the idea that there might be more to it than health and strength.

'Why would he need to be anything more? He has nothing to do with bringing up the baby elephants. In fact, he's kept well away from them by the females.'

'Doesn't he even have to be clever?'

'Clever enough to choose a suitable female and persuade her to have his baby; and clever enough to survive until he's old enough to do that. That's all. The female elephants supply all the other cleverness that's needed to make sure that the herd survives.'

'So where do the Seven Tests come in – what did you call them, the Mihitami Saba?'

'The Mitihani Saba. They come in right about here, where I am now, at twelve years old. I have to prove that I'm capable of looking after myself, and that I can do some of the things that male elephants do. Then for the next twelve years I do them. After that I can think about finding a female.'

'If you pass the tests what do you get?' Sheena was thinking of Boy Scout badges.

'I get Accepted. I can mix with the other young males when I want to. I can watch, and learn, how things are done. I can get ready.'

'Get ready for what?'

'I've told you – being a father.'

'You mean having babies. That's not being a father.'

But for the elephant it was. There was nothing else.

Sheena thought that sounded rather circular, and sad. She just hoped that the things the elephant would do, as he spent the next twelve years walking slowly around the circle from being a baby to making one, were enjoyable.

Suddenly their conversation was interrupted. There was a trumpeting in the distance, far over the trees and away from the river bed. It was loud. It must have been very loud at the place it was coming from. It had to be an elephant.

'It's time,' said the elephant, turning towards the sound. He sounded anxious. 'It's time for Mtihani wa Buri. The Test of the Tusks.'

Chapter Four: Mtihani wa Buri

Sheena was travelling again, not wrapped in the elephant's trunk this time but sitting on his head.

She felt reasonably safe up here. His head was slightly domed, and she was well settled, partly behind the dome. Whenever he lifted his head, though (which he did every now and again in order to lift his trunk also and sniff the air), she started to slide backwards and down onto his thick neck, and she had to brace herself with her hind legs then push herself back into position.

She didn't feel sick this time, in spite of the sway. She wondered whether elephants themselves ever felt queasy, moving as they did like slow boats in a heavy sea, up and down, side to side, all the time. In despair after Dad Allen's first few jokes, Thomas had taken over from him.

'What do you give a seasick elephant?'

'Lots of room.'

Only Mum Allen had laughed that time, however, and Thomas had decided there and then that most of the elephant jokes he knew were unfunny and out-of-date, so he had begun to construct his own series of elephant-and-computer jokes.

'What do you do to protect the floor when an elephant's going to be sick?'

'Open a spreadsheet under the elephant.'

'What do you make sure the spreadsheet has?'

'Very wide margins.'

'What do you get on the spreadsheet when the elephant is sick?'

'Feedback'.

They had not set off straight away. It seemed Mpole (they had settled on that shorter name for him) wanted to be gradual about Mtihani wa Buri, whatever that particular test consisted of.

Sheena felt altogether better, and her eyesight was much clearer. Before Mpole lowered his trunk so that she could climb up it onto his head, she had been able to examine him closely, and had realised how very approximate, until now, her impression had been of what an elephant looked like. Amy and Thomas had attempted a competition, during the journey, to see who could draw the best elephant, but the bumpiness of the road had soon forced them to give up. Thomas had taken the opportunity instead to come up with another joke.

'How do you use a graphics program to draw an elephant?'

'Select grey as the foreground colour and use the eraser tool to remove everything that doesn't look like an elephant.'

Sheena didn't think that either Thomas's or Amy's drawing would have come close to what she could now see. There was so much sharp detail within Mpole's loose elephant shape that Sheena had never noticed when she was watching wildlife programmes alongside the family – wrinkles in various criss-cross patterns, all over his body; surprisingly long, strong, black eyelashes; toenails set neatly into his rounded feet. His trunk opened up at the end into what looked like two pale pink lips. His mouth had its own lower lip, which was triangular and pointed outwards and downwards, but without pouting – in what was nearly a smile, in fact. His tail was quite long, covered in bristles, and curved jauntily upwards.

They had talked some more. Sheena had told the elephant she needed to get back to where the Allens had pitched their tents. She badly wanted some reassurance after her ordeal – reassurance that the family were still there, reassurance that they hadn't had any trouble with spitting cobras or anything remotely like them, reassurance that the Land Rover still had four wheels which could eventually take them all back to a safer place.

Not that she was in a hurry to leave Baragandiri. Her spirits had recovered along with her body, and she now felt she was up to another adventure or two – as long as no spitting was allowed. She had to touch base first, however, and maybe touch Amy's hair while she was sleeping, even risk a quick snuffle in her ear. She needed to look for some food, also (Mpole had provided her with more water, and she had very wet fur to prove it).

So she had said, 'Well, then, I'll be on my way.'

The elephant was silent. Sheena was puzzled.

'Is that alright? I mean, do you mind?'

'No, don't mind.'

He was not convincing.

'Is there something you want me to do? Something you want me to help you with?'

There was more silence. Then the elephant said, all of a whoosh, 'The tests I want you to help me with the Seven Tests they're going to be very hard will you?'

Sheena saw for the first time how worried the young elephant was by what lay ahead of him.

'Wouldn't that be cheating? I mean, is it allowed? How could I help you anyway? I'm only a little cat, and your tests are bound to be very big.'

'You could help me because I *am* a polay elephant. *Gradual* does sound better; but *polay* mainly means *slow*. I think slowly.

'To pass the tests you sometimes have to think quickly. I can't do that. But *you* can. You're *kasi* – quick...quick in the brain.'

'I can't do your thinking for you: that *would* be cheating. It might help you to get through the tests, but it wouldn't help you to *feel* that you'd got through them – to feel that *you*'d got through them, I mean.'

Sheena was using her kasi brain to think quickly. She tried to imagine hiding behind the elephant's ear and whispering answers to difficult questions or instructions about how to solve difficult problems. She couldn't see how that would work. Besides, wouldn't the tests be mainly physical – rolling rocks and tearing up trees and so on?

'I know that. I have to prove who I am, as well as what I can do. But it would be good to have you around. You could talk to me a bit, tell me how you think I'm doing and give me advice.'

Sheena thought some more. She had come to Baragandiri for new adventures. Here was a chance for some, and it didn't seem that they would involve any danger. More importantly, Mpole had saved her life, and risked his own to do it. She wanted to help him if she could. Maybe, if she couldn't do his thinking for him, she could help him *to* think: there was an important difference, one Dad Allen had talked about when he'd been complaining that some of his students (he taught Economics in the Secondary School) were using scientific calculators to do their work for them, in ways which hid the fact that they might not be able to do it by themselves.

It all ended up with Sheena riding the elephant's lumpy head towards Mtihani wa Buri, which seemed as if it would take place some way off: they had crossed the dry bed of the Ubi River and walked alongside it for a while, then away from it.

Sheena knew that she was breaking her promise to stay and look after Amy and Thomas; and the boap was a big one. She tried not to think about it as they moved steadily through the mixture of trees, following the line of the river. While they travelled Mpole told her about the test.

'It's just a sort of fight, really, or rather a kind of wrestle. I have to wrestle the smallest of the Accepted elephants, by locking tusks with him. It's like being on a steep track, going upwards, with all the male elephants on it one above the other. You start at the bottom and work your way up. If I beat this elephant I can take his place and challenge the next biggest. That would be for another day of course. Mtihani wa Buri is just to see if I can get onto the beginning of the track.'

'And what will I be doing – holding your wrinkly coat while you fight?

'Why are elephants wrinkled, anyway?' she asked him, trying to lighten his mood.

'I...er...don't know.'

'Because they're very difficult to iron.'

'Oh.' For an elephant Mpole's voice could sometimes be very small.

'Was that a test?'

'No,' Sheena said, 'it was joke' (and it helped explain why Thomas had decided to create some new ones. Mpole had if anything become even gloomier.)

'You needn't do anything, except climb up a tree so that you'll be safe, and watch. Then when it's all over you can tell me what you think – how I could have wrestled better, and so on. That will be very useful when I do the test again.'

'What makes you think you'll have to do it again?'

'I just think it. I think I'll fail.'

'Then you've failed already. Part of the test, of all the tests, will be seeing if you believe you can pass them.'

'There you are – you're thinking better than me already. Thank you for sticking with me!'

'Sticking *on* you, you mean! It's not easy up here. Why do you keep lifting your head and sniffing like that, with your trunk?'

'To smell who's there already, at the Fighting Space. I can smell that most of the Accepted Ones are – the younger ones, that is. They're the ones who'll be watching. Not far now.'

Before long they came to a wide clearing, bounded on one side by another stretch of sand river – perhaps the Ubi still, if it had curved round this far.

'Now's a good time for you to jump down.'

That wasn't so easy. Mpole wasn't a big elephant, but from the top of his head the ground seemed a long way.

Mum Allen had decided at one point in the journey that she

might as well make a contribution to the elephant-and-computer jokes (partly to show Thomas and Amy that she was really quite a Modern Mum).

'When would you look for an elephant with a computer monitor on his head?'

'On a hot day, when you wanted a high screen.'

Sheena found the best way to get down to ground level was to turn and run along the elephant's backbone to where it sloped down over his rump. The wrinkles in his skin made it easy for her to maintain her grip, even when the slope became steep. ('Good job elephants don't *get* ironed!' she thought), and she was able to come close to the ground before she had to leap down onto it.

There was a large tree at the edge of the clearing, and she decided it would be a good idea to climb it, since it seemed that big things were about to happen at ground level. She scrambled up easily. There were lots of large sausage-shaped fruit hanging from the branches. Thomas had shown some interest when he learned that sausage-trees grew in Baragandiri, and wanted to know if there were mashed potato trees as well. These fruit, however, were green, very hard, and more like suspended torpedoes than sausages.

She could now see down into the clearing.

Sheena had wanted to see elephants. Now she saw them in abundance. There were twenty or thirty already there, and some were still making their way through the trees.

'How do you get lots of male elephants to come together at the same time?'

'You use male-merge.'

There was a group of four or five in the middle of the clearing. Mpole walked straight towards them, and the smallest of the group stepped forward to meet him. Smallest, but still bigger than Mpole, and with longer, thicker tusks.

There was no ritual involved, no introductions or waving of trunks to a trumpeting crowd. They got straight to it.

Well, not quite straight. The two elephants came at each other from a slight angle, so that their tusks slipped under and over each other. (They had lifted their trunks out of the way.) Then they began to shove and twist, as if each was trying to unscrew the other's head. Sometimes they backed off, shook their heads violently, then came together again with a clatter of ivory. As they twisted they moved round in a circle, and dust rose from beneath their shuffling feet.

The other elephants hardly moved. Most were standing sideways, watching out of large, still eyes.

Mpole appeared to be doing very well: whenever he had been pushed backwards he forced his way forwards again. It was hard to tell, as the two large heads twisted first one way then the other, who had actually done the twisting in each direction. There were pauses during which they stood head to head, tusks still interlocked, and nothing seemed to be happening. Only the muscles bulging on their necks showed that they were still straining against each other. During those pauses they looked like a pair of large book-ends in training.

'How will they know who's won?' Sheena wondered.

'How will you know who's won?' she whispered down from the tree. The two elephants had broken away from each other. The larger one had walked back to the small group it had been with earlier. Mpole had come over to stand under Sheena's tree, as if he was not allowed to go near the others. The contest didn't seem to be over: the other elephants were still waiting, and watching.

'One of us will get tired.'

Mpole made no effort to speak quietly. He didn't seem to care much whether Sheena was seen or not. Did he want it to be known that he had at least one friend in the world, small and strange-looking though she might be?

'He'll be pushed backwards and won't be able to come forward again. His head will droop because his neck will have lost its strength. He may even fall, and that will be the end of it. Either way, he'll know he's beaten. Everyone will know. Then he'll walk away.'

Sheena found the fact that Mpole said 'one of us' and 'he', rather than 'I', hopeful. He seemed to be getting on better than he'd expected, and there was a bit of a gleam in his dark eye.

'I've noticed something about the other elephant,' Sheena said. 'When you aren't pushing hard against each other he lifts his left back leg and swings it, as if he's trying to loosen it up. I think it's hurting him. You might be able to use that.'

'How?'

Sheena had some ideas, but she wasn't saying. She really believed what she'd told Mpole, that he needed to think his own way through things if he was to come out of the other side of the test with the feeling that he had got there by himself.

'Maybe if I pushed suddenly while his foot was off the ground like that I could take him by surprise.'

'Maybe. It's worth a try.'

Mpole did need *some* help: he was younger, lighter, less confident; but that was as far as she would let her coaching go – observation > question > encouragement, with no actual instructions. What did a cat know about wrestling, anyway? She hadn't done any since she was a bouncy kitten, and that was a long time ago and a long way away, and then her mother had been killed and the litter was split up and she had got lost and life had suddenly become a struggle of a different kind…

Mpole walked back into the middle of the clearing. The other young elephant was already there.

The plan worked too well. The two elephants locked tusks again and strained against each other, their rear legs straight, the front half of their bodies lifting with the force of the push. Then there was a slackening, a slight movement backwards, a slight drop of the bodies, and the other elephant's foot came up off the ground. Mpole lunged suddenly, their two foreheads crunched together, and the bigger elephant was forced backwards, and backwards, and backwards, one slow step at a time.

There was a stir among the watching elephants, and Sheena scrambled up higher so that she could see better.

Then, disaster. The two pairs of tusks slipped against each other and Mpole lurched forward. One of his opponent's tusks raked down the side of Mpole's chest and gashed it open. Blood began instantly to pour out onto his right leg, a smooth red stream running down over the rough and dusty grey skin.

The two elephants broke apart. The larger one stood still. Mpole walked around in a circle while the blood continued to run.

'That's it. He's lost. I hope he'll be alright.' Sheena said to herself.

She mainly meant alright as far as his chest was concerned; but she also, partly, meant alright as far as losing was concerned.

He did not seem to be seriously injured, however. He was walking freely enough. After a short while and as he moved around the clearing (with the other elephants watching even more closely) the trickle of blood slowed and darkened and lost its glisten. He stopped under Sheena's tree once more.

'Oh dear! Are you alright?' she asked.

'Yes, alright. Hurts a bit. Won't be a problem.'

'Does it mean…er…you'll have to take the test again?'

Sheena carefully avoided the words 'failed' and 'lost'.

'No. Not finished yet.'

To her surprise he turned and walked back to where the other elephant was still standing. Maybe showing your toughness was an important part of Mtihani wa Buri, even if you did lose in the end.

The next round (that's what this wrestling match was breaking up into, a series of rounds) was straightforward. The two contestants walked directly forward into each other and came together with what would have been a clang if they'd been made of metal. There was no twisting this time, just shoving. Mpole didn't start bleeding again; and the other elephant didn't lift its rear leg again: it knew better than to do that. Mpole was being pushed gradually backwards, the other elephant's greater weight having its inevitable effect.

'What now?'

Mpole was back under the tree. Sheena thought he was beginning to look despondent. He had finally managed to stop his opponent pushing him backward, but only just; and another pause had come.

'You can't win this just by shoving. He's heavier than you. And you can't win it by twisting. He's stronger. That's how the land lies.'

'I don't understand.'

'*That's how the land lies* means, *That's how things are, and you have to make the best of them*. Maybe you should think about how the land *does* lie.'

The clearing was fairly level, but just in front of the sausage tree there was a sharp dip.

'Here's something else for you to think about. Dung beetles.'

The last time she was in Baragandiri she had watched dung beetles, shiny blue-black insects with flattish foreheads and spiky legs. They were working near a large, steaming elephant dropping (that was the nearest Sheena had got to elephants, on that first safari). One end of the dropping had come apart as it fell, and had opened up into a pile of moist gold-coloured straw with lots of bits in – twisted and half-digested leaves, a twig or two, seeds, some tiny pebbles. The dung beetles had scratched out select portions of the enormous heap, and using all six of their legs had shaped them into balls.

One of them began rolling its ball away, presumably towards a nest somewhere. Sheena had no idea what it would do with the dung once it got it to the nest, but she was fascinated by the insect's strength (the ball was twice as big as the beetle), its perseverance (it just kept going, even over the roughest patches of earth) and the skill with which it controlled the whole process.

It was using the lie of the land – dribbling this massive, squidgy football, giving it a little sideways nudge every now and again to make sure it followed a downward path, digging its legs in to slow the ball down when it began to gather speed in a wrong direction, and then re-directing it.

At one point the ball rolled into a hollow and stopped. The beetle tried pushing it from behind, but it wouldn't go over the forward lip of the hollow. The beetle then came round to the front of the dung-ball, braced itself against its roundness (standing almost upright) and scratched away some earth with its rearmost legs. Then it suddenly jumped to one side and the ball, as if taken by surprise, rolled forward, bounced out of the dip and continued its downward movement. The beetle had to skitter downhill, pounce on the dung-ball, and roll over with it several times before it managed to get it under control once more.

Elephants should know all about dung beetles: they were important to each other. Elephants pooped a great deal – many times a day and in large volume. The Allens had done some serious research on elephants in preparation for this safari. The research had consisted of watching lots of wildlife dvds. Sheena, settled on a comfy seat, had watched with them.

Elephants, the family learned, were very impressive in the matter of poo. They dropped as many as twelve loads a day – anything up to a hundred kilogrammes total, said the female narrator on one dvd. She had a posh voice which Mum Allen said sounded a bit sniffy, as if the narrator didn't think it was quite proper to talk about poo (which she had called 'excreta').

'Well, it's altogether a sniffy subject,' said Dad Allen. That encouraged Thomas to add his own contribution to the discussion, a pre-journey elephant joke.

'What sound does an elephant make as it walks through the jungle?'

'Gedung, gedung, gedung.'

By carrying the dung to new places, the beetles helped spread the seeds that had passed through the elephants' digestive system (without being digested). They also enriched the soil, fed other insects, and all in all helped the whole area to regenerate. Eventually there would be more trees for the elephants to feed from; and since that would allow more elephants to live there…

The important question for the moment, however, was whether Mpole had watched dung beetles at work. Had he learnt anything from them about how to use force creatively and not just blindly, in a straight shove?

Sheena watched anxiously as Mpole walked away from the tree, then around in circles. He was obviously thinking hard; but she knew that things would be happening only very gradually in his large head.

Then he came back to the far edge of the dip in the ground, and stopped with his back to it. The other elephant had to come over to join him so that they could begin their contest once more. Soon they were head to head again, pushing, pushing, pushing, with neither giving way.

Just when it seemed as if they had turned to stone, Mpole moved suddenly sideways. The other elephant was still in the middle of its great shove, and lurched forward. Its right leg went down into the dip, it lost its balance, then it half-tipped, half-rolled into the hollow. It fell onto its side. Its grey belly wobbled like a water balloon, then settled.

A cloud of dust rose into the air and drifted towards the elephant group. They were very still; Mpole had stopped moving; and the fallen elephant lay where it had crashed.

It's a serious business for an elephant to fall. Its great weight means that it can do serious damage, not just to its legs (which can break easily in spite of their thickness) but to its internal organs. This one had the advantage of being young, and not so massive, but it was obviously a very unhappy animal. It panicked: elephants feel very vulnerable when they are down. It began to kick, squirm and struggle, and even squeal a little in a youngish sort of way. It eventually rolled over from its side onto its stomach. It paused, heaved itself up first onto its front legs and then, with great effort, straightened its back legs so that it was standing once more – still in the bottom of the hollow.

It showed no inclination to climb out. The fight was over. Mtihani wa Buri was over.

Mpole had begun to walk away. There was a kind of stiff-legged pride in the way he moved.

The other elephants started milling around in the clearing, and two of them came and stood under Sheena's tree so that she couldn't see a way of getting down and round them without being seen. She wanted to run after Mpole, who seemed to have forgotten about her.

'Hey, wait for me!' she started to shout, running out along the branch and dancing on it; but, remembering that she shouldn't be there, she stopped her shout before it came fully out. She didn't stop her dance in time, however. Her jumping caused one of the torpedo-like fruits to break off, and down it fell, taking her with it, onto the head of the elephant directly below.

The elephant probably never worked out how these two very different fruit came to bounce on its head and then onto the ground, nor how one of them, the black-and-white one, managed to jump up and race off through the trees on little legs.

Sheena didn't care one jot about the confusion behind her. She just ran.

Chapter Five: Mtihani wa Mteketezo

'So what will happen to the elephant you beat?'

Sheena had been relieved, and pleased, to find Mpole waiting for her a little way back along the river bank.

'Will he become Unaccepted?'

'No. Once you're Accepted you're Accepted for good – unless you do something really, really bad.'

Sheena wondered what 'really, really bad' was, for an elephant.

'He'll be able to challenge another elephant so that he can try to take its place and begin climbing the track again. But not me. For the moment he's the Futon Elephant.'

Futon? That was what Sheena liked to lie on when she was watching tv with the family – a kind of folded mattress that could be used as either a sofa or a bed. Then she realised Mpole meant 'Foot-on' – 'with one foot on the bottom of the track, below the lowest elephant'. Maybe her brain wasn't so kasi after all; but she'd been half-remembering some of Thomas's jokes:

'What's grey, soft and lumpy and lies around the house?'

'A futon elephant.'

'What's grey, soft and lumpy, lies around the house and can't be moved?'

'A fourton elephant.'

'Was that your first fight?'

'My first real fight. We have Mapanbano ya Kalasha when we're young – Small Tusk Fights. They're just play-fights.'

'Will you ever have to fight again?'

'I could be challenged by the next young elephant who wants to become Accepted. Or I could choose to fight my way up the track – the ranking. That would be good practice for when I'm older. Then I'll have to take part in Mapigano ya Mapusa – the Fights of the Large Tusks. They're to decide who will have the pick of the females. That's not until I become a Tusker, however – an elephant with big tusks.'

(Then a Hoover should be a horse with big feet, Sheena thought.)

'So what's next, for now?' Sheena wanted to know. She could see herself developing a taste for this test thing...but more particularly for this teaching thing. Not having had kittens of her own, she had never been called upon to teach anybody anything. Oh, she had tried to educate Toby about cat-lick protocol (e.g. that when a friend licks you you're supposed to lick them back, at least sometimes); and she had had to train Thomas in the fine art of chasing a cat when it wants to be chased. Neither of those was the same as helping somebody who needed to learn how to do something important – like think. So she had taken great satisfaction in leading Mpole towards a plan for winning the wrestling match.

'Leading', that was the key word. Dad Allen had muttered something about it when he had been struggling with an essay for his distance-learning Master's Degree in Education. 'Education', that was it, too: the word came from a Latin term, *educere*, meaning *to lead out*. Leading out was better than pushing out from behind. She would have had difficulty pushing Mpole anywhere from behind. So she had dangled a couple of ideas in front of him instead, and he had followed them.

'You mean what's the next test? Well, that's really up to me. I can do Mitihani Saba in any order. I decided to do Mtihani wa

Buri first because I was lonely. At least that test let me get close to other elephants for a while.'

'How long have you been on your own?'

'A month. It's a month since my mother drove me away. One day she suddenly said, "It's time." She spoke quietly, but I knew I had to go.'

'That was you being Sent Out?'

'Yes.'

There was once a time when Dad Allen insisted on Putting the Cat Out, as he called it. It seemed that was one of the rituals a father had to perform before he Locked Up for the Night. She had hated being Put Out (she was very put out about it, in fact), but she always knew she'd be Let In again in the morning. Mpole's problem seemed much more permanent.

'So you can't be with other elephants now?'

'Not until I'm Accepted. It's not really a rule, it's just a fact. The other young males won't have anything to do with me until they know I'm worth having something to do with. That's where the Seven Tests come in.'

'So what *will* the next one be, for you?'

'I've been thinking hard about that.'

(That was a good sign.)

'I've decided it will be Mtihani wa Mteketezo – the Test of the Great Fire.'

Sheena had heard of that sort of thing. Primitive societies used to have Fire Tests. Young men had to walk on red-hot coals with their bare feet, or climb a tree which was then set on fire below them: they needed to reach the top before the fire did, and jump off.

Some of the boys in Thomas's year group, for *their* Fire Test, had had to smoke a whole packet of cigarettes, one after the other, without being sick, before they were allowed to join a gang they wanted to belong to. That was a bit primitive too, Sheena had decided.

'We have to walk through the Wall of Flame and across the Black Ground.'

'That seems a bit pointless to me. I can understand why you need to prove you can fight, so Mtihani wa Buri made a kind of sense. But when would you ever have to walk through a wall of flame?'

Dad Allen had once said that he was against testing for the sake of testing. (Thomas had said that he was against tests.) Sheena agreed with Dad Allen. Testing was important, but life provided quite enough real tests of its own.

'Elephants have to, sometimes, even though we're frightened of fire.'

'How did the elephant get into the computer?' Thomas had asked.

He had had to answer himself: *'It looked for a crack in the firewall then minimised itself and clicked Enter.'*

He had tried again. *'What do you call an elephant that hides in a computer and causes problems?'*

Dad Allen found the answer that time (*'A Trojan elephant'*) and came back with one of his own (*'Where should you send a Trojan elephant?*) which only Mum Allen could work out the answer to (*'Into elephantine quarantine'*).

'Is that the same as *tembo limbo*?' asked Dad Allen. Sometimes he and Mum Allen took over the children's games and had some fun of their own. On that occasion the fun was a bit too clever for Amy and Thomas, who therefore sulked.

'Hunters light fires in the long grass to make us run towards where they're hiding with their guns,' Mpole continued. 'Then they shoot us. For our tusks.'

Sheena knew that.

'And the best way to escape – the only way to escape – is through the fire.

'There's a fire burning at the moment, up towards the Sangando Hills. I could be there by this afternoon.'

'Why would you go there, if there are hunters?'

'Oh no, there are no hunters. That fire has been set by the Park Rangers, mainly to encourage new grass to grow so that the grazers have plenty to feed on. Keeping the grass short also makes it easier for Park visitors to see the animals. Poachers aren't a problem up there – it's too close to the Sangando Guard Post.'

'Alright, I'll come.'

Sheena hadn't waited to be asked.

'Will the other Accepted Ones go with you, to watch?'

'No, there's no need for that. There are always one or two elephants up there (there are always one or two elephants everywhere, although you may not see them). The news will get back about how I've done.'

Sheena didn't see how she could be much help to Mpole in the Test of the Great Fire. All you had to do was put your head down and run, surely, and hope that you avoided the three Bs – Blistering, Boiling and Bursting into Flames. She herself was terrified of fire, had had a very bad experience with it when she was a kitten; but she assumed she'd be able to do what she had done during Mtihani wa Buri – climb a tree and watch from a safe distance.

The fire had been burning for several days. Sheena could smell it when they were only half-way there. Mpole had been walking North for quite a long time. Sheena was comfortably enthroned on the young elephant's head, except when he stopped to sniff the air – then she was in danger of being deposed, or rather deposited. They hadn't had to pass close to Tembo Campsite, so her boap feeling had remained weak.

When they came out from the trees they had travelled through much of the way, she could see hills ahead of them, and a long line of smoke stretching across the open grassland off to the right. Small flames flickered at ground level. It wasn't anywhere near as dramatic as she had expected.

'That's not much of a fire. Where's the Wall of Flame?'

'We must walk closer, and wait.'

They walked closer, and waited. Sheena used the time to hunt out a couple of luncheon mice. Mpole had a long drink from a small pool at the edge of a deep muddy pit. The water level went down noticeably each time he slurped.

She, too, drank, to wash down the mouse fur that had got stuck in her throat. Then she drank some more, since it was a while since she'd been near water. Then she drank some extra more, since she didn't know when they would be near water again.

'What's the plan?' she asked.

'We wait a little longer. The fire will come to us soon. The wind begins to blow strongly about this time, nearly every day.'

The smoke had not come any closer since they stopped. Now, though, Sheena felt a freshening of the wind, and the smell sharpened. The flames at the base of the smoke began to get taller, and were soon showing much further up through the drifting greyness. The grass between here and there was long, and there were lots of dry-looking bushes scattered among it.

But no trees. When Sheena looked around for a tree to climb and be safe in, there were no trees. She began to panic.

'There are no trees! How am I supposed to stay out of the fire if there are no trees? I don't need to pass Mtihani wa Mteketezo! Let me out!'

'But what good would a tree do you, little cat? Trees burn too, you know.'

'I'll go back then. I'll just go back and wait for you. Good luck!'

She turned to run.

'You can't. Look!'

When she looked again she saw that the flames were now very high, surging as if they were bright orange waves, their crests flicking lines of smoke up into the air like slow black whips that shed golden sparks as they were cracked. She could hear the cracking, and the more constant crackling that went with it. The wind had begun to blow fiercely, and the fire was moving towards them very quickly. If she ran, it would catch up with her in no time.

'So what's Plan B?'

'It's Plan A. And it's what it always was – to walk through the flames. That's what I'm supposed to do. There's no way of escaping them now.'

'That's all very well for you: you've got a fire-resistant skin. But I'm flammable. We need to turn Plan A into Plan A With Knobs On. We need to think.'

That was what she'd promised to help Mpole do anyway, wasn't it? But now they were going to have to do some thinking for both their sakes, not just his. They weren't just facing a test, they were in a Situation.

She knew that the worst thing you can do when you're in a Situation is Panic. She'd already felt the beginnings of panic when she had realised she was treeless. Panic stopped you from thinking.

'Don't panic. Stay cool!' she told herself.

'Stay cool!' she told Mpole. She thought he must be starting to panic as well.

'What do you give an elephant who's starting to panic?'

'Trunquillizers.'

'Why did the elephant who had taken too many trunquillizers put his head down on the computer keyboard?'

'He had gone into sleep mode.'

Thomas's jokes kept coming into her head at very inappropriate moments. The flames were now roaring towards them.

'I know how to stay cool!' Mpole said; but he meant the physical kind of cool.

'We sometimes cover ourselves in mud to stop the sun from burning our skins. That might work for fire as well!'

Flame-block! Why hadn't Sheena thought of that! There was a big tub of mud right next to them!

Mpole led the way, down into the slippery sludge. Sheena had done something like this before, when she had impersonated a pangolin, and she didn't hesitate to follow the elephant into the mud-hole. She wriggled and rolled in the slurping mass, stretched and squirmed in it. It was so thick that she did not feel in danger of sinking any further into it.

'Mud, mud, glorious mud! Nothing quite like it for cooling the blood!'

She hoped the song that Dad Allen sometimes sang in the bath would turn out to have some truth in it. In other circumstances this might have been fun. She even tried singing the song herself, to lighten the moment. Then Mpole darkened it by rolling on her.

She wasn't expecting that; and she wasn't expecting the mud

to be so deep. She was pressed right down into it by the great weight of Mpole's body. Everything went dark, and silent. She struggled to get out from under him, struggled against the pressure of the mud that held her tight from every side. How far down was she? She had no way of knowing. How long before she drowned? Not long.

Mpole couldn't know that she was there, underneath his bulk. When he stood up he would think she had just run away, against his advice.

He must have rolled back again in order to climb out of the mud-hole, for the great weight pressing her down was suddenly lifted. She kicked and twisted towards the air; but where *was* the air? Which way was up? For all she knew she might be struggling further down into the dark and choking morass.

Then she felt the tip of Mpole's trunk moving over her body. More of his trunk wrapped itself around her middle and she was pulled, slurpingly, out of the deep slime and set down in the shallower mud at the edge of the hollow. She gasped, and spluttered mud in all directions.

'Sorry! Didn't know I'd done that! Good job you gurgled: a bloop of air came up to the surface and I knew you must be down there somewhere.'

Sheena had had a nasty shock.

'Mud, mud, horrible mud! Nothing quite like it for changing the mood!' she thought.

Now there was no time to waste, no time to let the first coat dry and apply a second one. They clambered out of the mud hollow side by side. Mpole looked like a chocolate elephant, a sort of very large Easter treat.

'We need to hurry!' said Sheena. She couldn't give Mpole time to work out for himself that they had to get through the flames while the mud was still wet. Sometimes the best kind of teaching was telling.

She did waste some time, however, trying to climb up Mpole's trunk onto his head. She and the trunk were entirely covered in slippery mud, and she slid back down onto the ground three times before Mpole curled his trunk around her and lifted her up where she needed to be. (He squeezed her too tightly the first time and she shot out sideways, plop onto the ground once more.)

But *was* that where she needed to be? As soon as he lumbered forward into a fast walk she started to slide from side to side, then she felt herself slipping backwards onto his neck. Soon she would be back on the ground again.

Mpole slowed down while they considered alternatives; but he had to keep moving towards the flames. He showed himself as good as Sheena at suggesting possibilities. 'Lateral thinking,' Dad Allen would have called it – 'thinking sideways'; and Sheena was quite impressed.

'Why don't you travel sideways?' said Mpole. 'You could hang on behind my ear and I could fold it back so that you were behind it. That would give you some extra protection.

'Or you can hang from my tail if you like,' he said. 'You'd be behind me, and that would keep you from the worst of the flames.'

Sheena would be behind his behind, and well protected, certainly, since his behind was very large. She turned and looked at his tail, which right now was up in the air. It was short and bristly, and she didn't think she'd be able to hang onto it for long. She wouldn't be able to dig her claws into it, in fairness to Mpole. It also occurred to her that even if she could cling to it and swing along behind him, there could be an additional problem. Mpole might get carried away and break wind (elephants were mighty backwards trumpeters, particularly when they were excited). Thomas had some relevant jokes, which had got him into trouble with his parents:

'What's the difference between a pub and an elephant fart?'

'One's a bar-room and the other one's a bar-ROOM!'

'What do you need to do when the elephant using the computer next to yours breaks wind?'

'Open a new window.'

The additional problem really lay in the fact that Mpole's tail-wind might just be highly explosive, and a flying spark might well touch him off...So Sheena decided the ear option would be safer, and possibly pleasanter.

It did work well, to begin with. Sheena wedged herself behind his right ear. When he pressed it back against his skull a loose flap of skin hung down, like a little hammock, and it helped support her body. She felt quite safe in there – it was almost cosy.

'Hang in there!' said Mpole, and he began to walk faster.

The last thing Sheena had seen before she tucked herself away were the flames rising ahead of them, now undoubtedly a wall, a wall taller than Mpole, a great roaring wall that would very soon sweep over them. Dry bushes were exploding on either side. She could not have survived on Mpole's head: she would have flowered into flame in an instant.

Soon it was *too* cosy behind his ear: the hot, suffocating air wrapped itself around her and she had difficulty breathing.

Mpole himself was doing no better. The mud had provided some protection for a while, but now it was drying out and beginning to fall off in large chunks as he ran, exposing his sensitive skin (which wasn't fire-resistant at all) to the great heat.

He had a trick up his trunk, however. He put the tip into his mouth, and from the gurgling sound which followed Sheena realised he was drawing water up from the big load in his stomach he'd taken on board back at the pool. He lifted his trunk above his head and sprayed water over his back and his ears. Some of it even trickled down over his passenger.

'Oh bliss!' Sheena cried.

He did it twice more; but the heat was now so intense that the water evaporated immediately, and soon it was steam more than anything else reaching Sheena. Mpole himself was in pain.

'Help! I'm overheating! Got to use my ears! Sorry!' he gasped.

Sheena knew that an elephant's ears were what it used to control its temperature. There was a network of large veins running across them, just under the surface of their thin skin, and they worked like radiators to carry heat away from the elephant's body. Especially when they were flapped. An elephant that couldn't flap its ears very soon got too hot, even in everyday sunshine. No wonder Mpole now had to flap his.

When his ears swung outwards the first time Sheena felt herself falling, and just managed to hook her front claws into a fold of skin running along Mpole's neck. It was her turn to apologise.

'Sorry' she called out, swinging there, precariously.

She couldn't stay there, even though her claws in Mpole's neck didn't seem to be hurting him. There were flames all around them. She could feel the heat searing her. Scorching orange tongues licked up towards her back legs, which were hanging down below Mpole's neck. So when he flapped his ears backwards once more she lifted a leg, jammed its paw into the pouch of skin which had re-formed in the angle between ear and skull, and sprang up onto his head.

The mud up there was dry now, and it was easier for her to stay in place. Otherwise things weren't much better. It was no cooler for one thing. Then there was the smoke, great coughing black clouds of it which burnt her lungs and stung her eyes. (Her poor eyes! They had only just recovered from Swila's poison!)

All she could see in the darkness ahead of her was Mpole's straight trunk, pointing upwards. He must be breathing through it, must be reaching through the smoke to cleaner air. She needed some of that!

She scrambled forward and up, as if his trunk were a coconut tree. By a mixture of hugging and digging in with her claws she worked her way towards the tip. Her weight caused Mpole's trunk to sway wildly to begin with, and she had to hang on tight; but the air *was* clearer there, and she could begin to breathe again.

She could also see further ahead. There were no flames. They were through the flames. All that lay in front of them was a black waste land, an expanse of charred earth and wispy smoke.

'We're through! We're through!' she cried.

'But we're not over!' said Mpole, and she felt him begin to walk even faster.

Then she remembered that there were two parts to Mtihani wa Mteketezo. They had passed through the Wall of Flame, but only to emerge onto the Black Ground. She knew Mpole would have a problem.

Elephants' feet look hard and horny, but they aren't. Elephants can walk very quietly, in spite of their great size. That's because their feet aren't hard at all, but very soft. The soles are like thin cushions filled with jelly: they're made of fatty tissue which moulds itself to the shape of the ground underfoot and gives the elephant a very good feel for it and a very good grip on it. Their large, sensitive foot-pads are one of the reasons why elephants hardly ever fall, even when they're climbing up and down steep hillsides.

Large, sensitive feet are no good on hot earth, however. This earth was *very* hot. The fire that had passed over it had turned it into a dark plateau of smouldering ash. It was still glowing, in patches, and smoke was still rising from it – white smoke rather than black, but smoke nevertheless. Already Mpole was having to pick his feet up into a trot (difficult for an elephant). It was as if the very soil was burning, and it was burning as far as Sheena could see ahead. Before they got much further Mpole's feet would be fritters.

She could feel the panic rising in him now: his heart was pounding (the thumping reverberated all the way up through his trunk), his ears were flapping wildly (but could not do much to cool his feet) and she was being swung violently from side to side at the end of his trunk, which he was still waving high in the air. She felt like a little black-and-white signal flag which said, 'Help!'

Mpole cried out for help, too. She felt the sound passing up through his trunk before she heard it. It came out above her head as a little, frightened squeal which reminded her that Mpole was really quite young, and shouldn't have had to do this, and needed his mother, who wasn't there.

She wasn't there: so Sheena had to do something. She remembered the water hole Mpole had kicked in the sand.

'Think water holes!' she cried. 'Think kicking!'

The crust of burning earth might not be very thick. If Mpole could only scrape through the surface to the cooler soil beneath, they might have a chance.

Then she fell. One of the sideways swings of Mpole's trunk was more violent than any that had gone before, and shook her loose. She bounced off his head, slid down his shoulder, and landed paws down on the hot black ash.

She immediately felt what Mpole must be feeling, and knew why he had started to run. Her paws were every bit a sensitive as an elephant's, and the pain that quickly came up through them was agonising. She jumped as high as she could, but the pain had hardly diminished before she landed and it began again, worse than before. She tried skipping on the spot, but although that meant that at least two of her paws were off the ground at any one time they were not in the air long enough to even begin to cool down.

She knew then that her feet were going to burn off and there was nothing she could do about it. She had long been used to having a stump as a tail. But stumps as legs?

Mpole had carried on running and was now well ahead of her. She couldn't have expected him to stop and pick her up; but she wasn't even sure he knew she had fallen off.

Then he suddenly slowed. 'Is he coming back for me?' Sheena thought.

He did not turn, however. He stopped, facing forwards, and started kicking the ground with his front feet. He had heard her before she fell, and her idea had gradually come to mean something to him, and he was trying it, and it might work!

Sheena forced herself to skip towards him, trying to ignore the pain and concentrate on missing the patches of earth that were glowing red. Mpole was moving forward again, much more slowly.

'Follow my footsteps!' he cried. So he did know she was behind him on the ground, must know she was suffering as much as he was, would realise that she was in even greater danger.

How could she follow his footsteps? She couldn't take strides anywhere near a long as his.

Then she saw what he was doing. He kicked at the ground with his front left foot, clearing a space in the smouldering ash so that he could then place that foot on bare brown earth – bare, brown, cool earth. Then he kicked a bare patch with his right front foot, and put it down. He lifted his left front foot again and brought the rear foot on that side forward onto the cleared area. Then he kicked a new bare patch with his left front foot, placed that foot, lifted his right front foot and brought his right back foot forward. In that way he was able to make slow progress without having to step on any burning ground.

As he worked through his next set of four kicks and steps, his body rocked forward; he lifted one of his back feet and exposed the first bare patch he had made. Sheena abandoned skipping, gathered herself for a leap (even though that meant putting all four paws on the ground) and jumped onto the patch. It was cool! Or at least it wasn't hot!

All she had to do now was jump from footprint to footprint as if they were stepping stones. All Mpole had to do was maintain his slow, rhythmic pattern of kicks and steps.

It was a long time before they reached ground cool enough to stand on normally. Even then walking was painful for them both, and Mpole insisted in carrying Sheena on his head. She licked her paws as they travelled, and that was soothing. She would have liked to do the same to Mpole's great feet.

Chapter Six: Mtihani wa Simba

They spent the night among some trees not far beyond the Black Ground, near where, to the North, the hills began to rise. Walking on their scorched feet was painful, so they had soon stopped. Mpole lay down to rest, something elephants don't really like doing. Sheena curled herself up near him. She felt safer close to the grey mound of his body: the last thing she wanted was to have to jump up and run away on her sore paws from something snuffling at her in the darkness.

Her paws hurt, but were not blistered. Her fur was scorched brown in places, but not burnt away. She was glad for once that she had only a short tail: a longer one might have caught fire and burnt like a torch. (Have we told you yet how her tail came to be stumpy? Perhaps some other time.)

The sun had gone down behind the line of fire stretching across the horizon behind them. It had looked red and angry and beautiful, with black streaks of smoke drifting slowly up across its face as it sank into the darkness.

As they settled down for the night, Sheena and Mpole talked. They didn't talk much about the fire. They talked about their early years.

Their lives had been very different, as you might expect. Mpole had had a family. Sheena had had no-one for most of the first six months of her life. Then Dad Allen rescued her, sick, bedraggled and flea-ridden, from under his parked car one hot

Caribbean night. She had been so weak that she probably wouldn't have been able to move when he drove off, and might well have been crushed under the car's wheels.

Mpole had from the beginning been wonderfully well cared for – fed, protected, played with, taught things. Then it had all come to a sudden end when he was Sent Out. He and Sheena debated for a long time the question of whether it was better not to have, then find, or to have, then lose.

What was certain was that Sheena was in some ways better equipped to survive than Mpole, even in this environment which was home to him and strange to her. From a matter of weeks after her birth she had had to live on her wits and work things out; Mpole was now, at this later stage in *his* life, having to learn to think for himself.

'You did some really good thinking back there,' Sheena said – and she meant it.

'You've invented a way of walking on the Black Ground. That might save some elephant lives, one day.'

She knew Mpole wouldn't selfishly keep the discovery to himself, just so that other Singletons could not use it when they faced Mtihani wa Mteketezo. That wasn't how elephants did things. Every elephant herd had a store of accumulated knowledge and skills, and every member of the herd had access to it to help him or her survive. Most of it was passed on to the calves as they grew up…by some mysterious natural process, it seemed.

'Why do elephants have cracks between their toes?'

'To hold their library cards.'

Sheena didn't think so.

'What kind of books do elephants read?'

'E-books.'

'What do you call a group of smart elephants who read a lot of e-books to make themselves even smarter?'

'A nerd.'

That wasn't how it worked, either, Sheena was sure. The herd's most specialised knowledge was carried by the herd leader (always a female) called the Matriarch, often the oldest elephant in the group. She was the one who decided where the herd should travel, for instance, in its search for food and water, since she had the clearest memories of where those things could be found at different times of the year. She knew more than the other elephants about what plants and tree-bark to eat to cure particular sicknesses. She also had the greatest terror of men and their guns, and knew most about hunters' tricks; and she did her best to keep the herd well away from that source of danger.

This new skill that Mpole had acquired would be shared, passed on (somehow) and become a permanent part of elephant behaviour. Pachydermologists (people who study elephants) would 'discover' the behaviour in years to come, and write triumphant Papers about it, almost as if they themselves had invented it.

'It might be useful. But you helped me think it up. Just like you helped me to think up the idea of using mud to keep the heat of the fire away from my skin.'

That, however, had just been an extension of an old trick, and hardly qualified as an invention. Elephants had always used mud to protect themselves from the sun. (Always? Perhaps only since some clever elephant had thought of the idea – invented it. Everything was an invention, first time round.)

They also covered themselves in mud, Sheena knew, to keep insects away, and to rid their skin of burrs (sharp, hitch-hiking seeds) and ticks (sharp, blood-sucking parasites).

'Where do elephants go to for skin treatment?'

'To a pachydermatologist.'

That had been one of Thomas's favourites, among the 'old' elephant jokes; Amy had had to have it explained to her.

Now wasn't the time to talk about the next test. Sheena wasn't altogether sure that she wanted to know what it would be.

Now was the time to rest.

Next morning the sun came up yellow and bright in the opposite side of the sky, as if it had passed through a rain shower during its overnight journey and been washed clean of the smokiness.

There was no sign of the fire. It had perhaps died down or moved away. Mpole explained that even if it was still burning it would stop well short of the main track down from the Park Gate, where the rangers had cleared the ground of all vegetation in a line which would act as a fire break.

'They set fire to only one part of the Park at time, so that the animals have plenty of places to run to,' said Mpole.

So Tembo Campsite would not be in any danger.

Sheena now knew even more clearly than she had already done why animals were afraid of fire. It was a monster. She knew more clearly, too, what Panic was. It was the feeling that took over when you faced forces you knew you couldn't control and which might destroy you: it either made you run when you should be standing still, or caused you to stand still, frozen in fear, when you should be running.

She also knew more clearly what Thinking was, and in particular Thinking for Survival. It was using your brain to see how the world works, to understand its forces great and small so that you might learn *to* control them...and if you couldn't, and they were threatening you, so that you could find a way past or through them.

There was one force, however, which Mpole didn't seem able to either control or avoid. That was the force driving him on to the other five tests. He had to do them. 'Peer Pressure' is what Mum Allen would have called it (she taught Life Skills among other things). Peer Pressure was being squeezed from the sides by those around you, so that you were forced forwards. The other elephants expected; so Mpole must. There was no way past. The only thing he could do was find a way through.

Sheena did suspect, however, that there was a touch of Pride Pressure at work as well. Mpole was certainly very proud of having passed two tests, and of the thinking that had helped him to do so.

'I'll probably go for Mtihani wa Simba next,' he said. 'The Test of the Lions.'

'Er...what does *next* mean?' asked Sheena. She wasn't sure she was ready for a today sort of next, especially if it involved lions. She knew lions.

'It doesn't mean anything very precisely,' said Mpole.

'It means that next time I see some lions I'll do the test.'

'You mean any old lions will do?'

Actually, she hoped that if she was going to tangle with lions they'd be young ones. Nyanya, the Old One, had been wily and nasty and had had nothing to lose, which made her very dangerous.

'Yes. All I have to do is walk through them.'

Sheena was familiar with the word *all*. It was a word people employed to trick each other, a word you could use to pretend that something was very small when it was Very Big.

'All you have to do is clean up your room' (Mum Allen to Thomas).

'All I want for Christmas is five new dolls' (Amy to her parents).

'All you have to do is lend me Annie for a couple of hours so that we can play Ambush' (Thomas to Amy. Annie was Amy's favourite doll of all time. Ambush was Thomas's favourite game of the moment, and involved creeping up with his friends on an unsuspecting target and firing at it with catapults.)

Just and *only* were similar words to *all*.

'I just have to go through the middle of the pride, without stopping. It'll only take a moment.'

'*Just*? Surely lions are dangerous, even to elephants?'

'They can be, to very small elephants at least. To bigger ones too, if they're hungry enough. That's where the luck of the test comes in.'

Sheena didn't think tests should involve luck. Otherwise there was a chance they wouldn't be fair. She didn't want to be on the unfair side of a set of lion teeth.

'Don't you get to choose which lions?'

'No. Once I've decided on Mtihani wa Simba I have to use the next lions I see.'

'How about if I go ahead and make sure the next lions you see have fat stomachs?'

'That *would* be cheating; it would be known; and *I'd* know, I'd know that I hadn't done the test properly.'

That now seemed to matter a lot to Mpole – knowing exactly how well he'd done, which was in some ways more important than just doing whatever it was.

'You can't help me with choosing the lions; but you can still help me with thinking about them. Just in case the test begins to go wrong.'

Sheena knew about *just in case* as well. It often meant *since it's likely that (so and so will in fact happen)*.

'Take a book with you, just in case I'm a bit late' (Mum Allen to

Dad Allen, when she was going shopping and he was meeting her afterwards).

The lions weren't very far away. Sheena and Mpole had breakfasted (field-mice again for her, sweet, unburnt grass for him). They had drunk at another, very small pool (more of a puddle really), and he had helped her wash the remaining mud out of her fur.

'I'll just spray some water on you,' he said. She should have noticed the *just.*

'What does an airport maintenance elephant use to hose down an airplane?'

'A jumbo jet.'

Sheena was well and truly hosed down.

When she could breathe again she climbed up Mpole's trunk onto his head, from which she dripped water into his eyes and it served him right.

They set off in a direction that would keep them clear of the area that had been overrun by the fire. The ground would have cooled by now, but they had no wish to walk through the ashes of their awful experience.

Before long they turned South again and came to some straggly trees. The lions were just beyond, on the far side of another mud-pond, one that looked quite deep. There were four of them, all females, lying around the remains of a dead animal. Sheena couldn't make out what the animal had started out as, since it had ended up as no more than a broken skeleton with bits of skin attached. The lions had obviously eaten everything edible, and their great round bellies suggested that they couldn't have eaten any more anyway.

'That's that then,' said Sheena.

'This bunch won't give us any trouble, will they? A quick stroll past their left-overs and we can be on our way. That's Mtihani wa Simba done. Tomorrow's another day.'

She felt quite perky, now that she knew they'd had good luck with the lions.

The only movement from the lions, as Mpole walked steadily round the mud-hole towards them, was the twitch of an eyelid and the flick of a tail.

Then the situation changed. Without warning all four lions sprang up simultaneously and shot off in different directions.

'Gosh! We must look pretty scary!' thought Sheena in her buoyant mood. She liked being part of an outfit that could frighten lions into running away.

'Does that mean the test doesn't count?' she wondered. Mpole hadn't managed to walk through the group, as he was supposed to, before it became four individuals who obviously didn't want to be here any longer.

'That wasn't Mpole's fault!'

No indeed it wasn't. It was the fault of the very large lion that now walked in from the grassland beyond the trees. It was a male, with a great shaggy mane and powerful shoulders. This was a very poor swap, Sheena considered, for the four tame-looking females who had left so quickly and were already nowhere to be seen. This lion's stomach was not round and full. Mtihani wa Simba had suddenly become much more difficult. How do you walk through a single lion? How do you walk through a single lion who's very big and hungry?

Mpole had stopped in his tracks, understandably, and now stood still, swaying slightly, trembling a lot. The lion walked around the animal skeleton and its thin remnants of skin, sniffing at it. There weren't even the beginnings of a meal there for an animal as big as he was. He turned his great yellow eyes on Mpole. Mpole and Sheena were being confronted by another of the world's forces, a very powerful one; and it didn't take much thinking to understand how this one worked. It worked by taking what it wanted.

Even a lion this big, however, would not have considered attacking Mpole if there had been other elephants around.

'Where are the other elephants?' Sheena whispered. 'You said there were always other elephants around, watching the tests.'

'Not exactly. *Watching* sometimes just means *knowing about*; and *around* for an elephant can mean several miles away. I think we're on our own.'

The lion now began to circle Mpole, slowly, sizing him up. Big though the great cat was, he was not much more than half Mpole's height. Mpole's tusks, although not large, were sharp. Mpole turned as the lion moved slowly around him, making sure his tusks were always pointing towards the threat.

Sheena didn't know how she could help. She tried a cat-to-cat stare, but found herself drowning in the twin amber pools of the lion's eyes. There was just too much power there.

As long as Mpole could face the lion he was safe. A lion usually attacks back then front, bringing its prey down from behind then seizing its throat in a strangling bite. This one couldn't get behind Mpole to take hold of a rear leg; and in any case Mpole's neck would be much too thick for the lion to close his jaws around. Perhaps they were safe. (Sheena assumed that if Mpole was safe she would be: she had no intention of getting down from Mpole's head; in fact, she now realised that she had stuck her front claws into the dome of his forehead in order *not* to get down. She persuaded herself that that would help him concentrate.)

She had forgotten about lions and hippos, however. She was about to be reminded.

Hippos, like elephants, are usually too large for lions to tackle. The other problems they present are similar, as well – thick necks and big teeth (rather than tusks). But lions have developed (invented) a horrific technique for killing hippos that have strayed too far from their water holes. They jump up onto their backs, dig their claws in so that they can stay up there, and begin scratching. They scratch down into the hippos' thin skin and through to the flesh beneath. The hippos start to bleed, heavily. When the lions have done enough scratching they jump off, let the hippos run, follow, and wait.

The hippos, losing large amounts of blood, try to make their way back to their water holes. Sometimes they succeed. Sometimes, however, they become too weak long before then, fall (or are brought down) and become victims.

This lion knew that technique. What worked on a hippo might work on an elephant.

He sprang suddenly, not directly at Mpole but to one side, landing with a deep thud on the hard ground. Then he sprang again, before Mpole had a chance to turn. It was more a bounce than a jump, but it took him up onto Mpole's back, where he quickly turned so that he was facing forwards.

Sheena swung round on Mpole's head and found herself looking straight into the lion's jaws. He was so close that he could have leaned forward, snapped her up and crunched her like a starter before the main meal. But he paid no attention to her. He was working to maintain his balance as Mpole began to turn and twist…and trumpet – not a pitiful squeal like the one he had emitted as they crossed the Black Ground, but a much more grown-up sound, a mixture of fear and anger.

The lion, however, had sunk his long claws deep into Mpole's skin, and now he began to scratch.

Sheena watched in horror and from close range as the lion's claws sliced down into Mpole's flesh and the blood started to well out of the gashes and run down his sides. She could hear the sound, a kind of rasping, and smell the hot blood. And she could also smell Mpole's fear. All his twisting and turning was having no effect. The lion could not be shaken off, could not be stopped.

Sheena had to try. She gathered herself and sprang for the lion's eyes. But the lion was much too quick. A heavy paw flicked at her as she jumped, and swatted her sideways so that she flew through the air and landed hard several yards away, rolling onwards until she hit a tree stump.

Luckily the lion's claws had not ripped into her; but the breath had been knocked out of her little body, and the consciousness had been almost knocked out of her little head. By the time she knew where she was and was able to turn round and look at what was happening, the lion had started scratching again.

Mpole was now bucking wildly, trying to throw the lion off, reaching over backwards with his trunk towards his tormentor. But his trunk was not long enough to allow him to get a grip on the lion and pull it to the ground where it could be trampled.

'Remember the glorious mud!' Sheena cried out. 'Wallow in the hollow!'

The pool of mud that the lions had been lying next to was

wide and deep. Mpole spun around towards it, took a few quick steps to its edge, and toppled in. The lion went with him. There was a great 'Ker-Splat!' and they both disappeared.

Who could know what then went on in the depths of that brown other world? All Sheena could see was a slow swirl on the surface, as if this were a great cauldron of thick brown gruel being stirred by something far beneath. There was an occasional 'Gloop!' as a large bubble of air broke upwards. Once, eerily, a set of four flat-topped lumps emerged from the mud, paused, and sank again.

'Mpole's feet! He's upside-down!'

Then everything went still, and the surface settled into smoothness.

Sheena feared the worst. Unable to disentangle themselves from each other, both animals had suffocated – 'drowned' wasn't right, didn't convey the sense of smother that must have come as the thick mud poured down throats and into lungs. Sheena ran anxiously up and down the edge of the pit.

Suddenly there was movement again, and something broke through the brown surface just in front of her.

She stopped. It was the tip of Mpole's trunk. The two lips at the end opened pinkly, and a blast of exhaled air splattered a thick spray of mud over her where she had halted. Then there was a great sucking-in through the trunk, and a great stirring beneath it, and the elephant's heavy shape rose slowly from the depths as he walked up out of the pond, mud running thickly down his sides as if he was melting.

Mpole said nothing. Sheena said nothing. They turned together and left the scene, Mpole walking slowly and steadily, Sheena trotting along beside him. Behind them the surface of the mud pool settled into stillness once more.

Chapter Seven: Mtihani wa Land Rover

Mud had helped save Mpole from the fire and from the lion. Now it almost certainly saved him from bleeding to death. The sun was well up in the sky, and hot, and the thick sludge on Mpole's skin quickly dried into a hard poultice. There were some reddish stripes on his back where blood had soaked through from his wounds, but they soon turned from bright to brown. His back was encased in a protective plaster, and he did not seem to be in any pain.

'That should count as two tests – Mtihani Mawili,' Sheena said. 'There were two lots of lion, and the second one was a Lot of Lion.'

'*Mi*tihani Mawili', said Mpole. 'And no, that was only one test. I'm not even sure I passed it: that wasn't at all what was supposed to happen. The Accepted Ones will decide, when they know about it.

'In any case I still have four tests to do.'

'It was more than a test anyway. It was Real Life,' Sheena argued. The not fairness of the big lion's arrival troubled her. And surely no elephant herd would want its young males to be injured or killed during Mitihani Saba?

She didn't ask about what had happened in the depths of the mud. She didn't tell Mpole that when she saw his feet floating on the surface she thought he had died. She certainly didn't tell him that what had come into her head then had been one of the tiredest of Thomas's jokes (the whole family had groaned when he told it, and that pleased him):

'Why did the elephant paint the soles of its feet brown?'

'So it could hide upside-down in the chocolate mousse.'

She had even added, in her mind, a joke of her own:

'Why couldn't you see the other animal in the chocolate mousse?'

'Because it was lion under the elephant.'

She was a bit ashamed of all of that. Brains were strange things.

She hesitated to ask what the next test might be. The fight with the lion had really frightened her. Mpole deserved something much easier, next time.

'I need to find a Land Rover,' Mpole said as if she *had* asked.

'What a coincidence: *I* need to find a Land Rover too,' she said.

'I need to find a Land Rover with TZL 8046 on its number plate. I need to find a Land Rover with TZL 8046 on its number plate which will take me to where the only test I have to do is the crunch test, to see if my cat biscuits are fresh. How about you?'

'Any old Land Rover will do.'

Sheena immediately thought of the any old lion who had shown up for the last test. *Great White* was old – Dad Allen was proud of how old it was; but Sheena didn't think she wanted the Allen family mixed up in any of these Mitihani. They were turning out to be rather too serious.

'Why a Land Rover?' she asked.

'We have to make a Land Rover turn around and go back the way it came. That's the test – Mtihani wa Land Rover. It has to be a Land Rover because...well I suppose it's because that's the tradition. Land Rovers were the first cars to come here, the first cars elephants had to challenge. They're a part of elephant history.'

Challenge it, make it turn round and go back the way it came: Mpole was talking about Land Rovers as if they were a kind of animal.

Sheena could see why. It was hard to think of *Great White* as a sleek, powerful shark (which is how Dad Allen saw it in his less sensible moments); it was much easier to view it as a large, clumsy, grumbling land creature with a will of its own and a tendency to stop. Mum Allen had often described it, in fact, as a White Elephant – looked up to and looked after (by Dad Allen) as if it were an important religious symbol, but pretty useless, and big and costly to maintain.

'What's the difference between a Land Rover and an elephant?'

'A Land Rover doesn't have a trunk' (a Thomas joke).

'What's the difference between a Land Rover and a White Elephant?'

'None' (a Mum Allen sarcastic comment).

Sheena didn't want the Allens to be put in any danger; but it might be that this test would have some fun in it, and fun was what she had come to Baragandiri to look for and fun was what she hadn't had much of so far, what with all the poisonous spit and gooey mud and scorching fire and cat-swatting lions' paws.

Making a Land Rover turn around and go back the way it had come didn't seem as if it would be a matter of risk, either for its occupants or for Mpole (about whom she found she worried, a little).

More important than all of that was the fact that the longer she stayed away from Tembo Campsite, now, the more her boap hurt her. She would be very happy to find out that Amy and Thomas had been safe in her absence.

'I know where there's a Land Rover. If you can take me back to where I had my snake problem, I'll show you.'

She could always allow herself to have a little moi about the last bit.

Mpole carried her on his head back to the exact spot where she had been blinded by the spitting cobra. It was late afternoon by the time they got there. There were the marks of trampling in the sandy earth, but nothing else. Swila's remains had gone. Sheena remembered her feeling that the snake had slithered into her head. She shivered.

'This way,' she said quickly, and they moved away from the river bank towards where she knew the tents would be. She told Mpole to slow down. She was amazed at how quietly he could walk. She had known about elephant foot technology in theory, but here it was working in fact. As a stealth treader herself, she was impressed.

Soon she could see the white shape of the Land Rover through the trees.

'Would you mind waiting here?' she asked.

She trotted back along Mpole's spine and jumped down to the ground. He immediately began to explore the tufts of grass with his trunk, pull some of them up, and stuff them into his mouth. He was obviously happy to let her reconnoitre for a while.

She crept through the trees (feeling that she was making much more noise than Mpole had done, in spite of her small size) until she was at the edge of the campsite. The family weren't to be seen. She heard them, however, further up the river bank, not far. If they walked straight back to the tents from there, there was no danger that they would come across Mpole as he fed.

Sheena took the opportunity for a quick nose around the campsite – truly a nose, since she sniffed the pots (not washed up yet) to see what the Allens had had for lunch, went into the children's tent and snuffled into Amy's pillow and Thomas's socks (very briefly), trotted over to the Land Rover and inhaled the vapours from its engine – partly as an antidote to the socks and partly to see, from how warm the engine was, whether it had been used recently. It hadn't.

So there was a good chance that the family would be going off soon for their Sundowners at the Lodge. (Sheena had by now worked out what Sundowners were. When Dad Allen was on holiday, she had remembered, he liked to drink a toast to the day just gone, and then to the day to come, which he knew would be even better.)

'Do you know the way to the Lodge? That place where people stay when they don't have tents?'

She was back with Mpole, who was still eating. She had heard the family returning to the campsite, with a discussion of the 'Yes you did...No I didn't' variety going on between Amy and Thomas, so she had crept away through the bushes.

'Yes. It's not far. Why?'

'I think the Land Rover will be going there soon.'

If Mpole did think a Land Rover was an animal, with a mind of its own, that was fine. It might keep the test simple. So she didn't explain about the family and her place in it.

'Very good,' said Mpole. 'We can take a short-cut over the high ground and get on the track ahead of it. This should be easy.'

Sheena wasn't so sure. What Mpole didn't realise was that if this particular Land Rover *was* a sort of creature it was one with five brains that often disagreed enormously with each other. She wanted to position herself where she would be able to hear the family talking as Mpole did his thing.

His 'thing' would be a series of mock charges, each one more ferocious than the one before, designed to stop, frighten, turn, chase. All elephants needed to be able to perform mock charges, as a way of protecting themselves and other elephants without getting into unnecessary danger or actual conflict.

Sheena knew that a mock something was a substitute for a real something: it was a pretence in the same way that a test was. Mock was fine, pretend was fine: she had had enough of real for a while.

They hadn't gone far from the campsite (with Sheena on Mpole's head once more) when they heard the unmistakable sound of the Land Rover starting up – a strained choking and churning, then a roar.

'What do a Land Rover and an elephant have in common?'

'One starts with a roar, the other one…'

Thomas had waited until Amy asked, eventually, 'What *does* the other one do?' Then he told her. She complained to their parents.

Mpole had to hurry over the rise and down towards the track. He chose a spot where it climbed up from the river valley, then turned and faced back towards the campsite. There was a bend just ahead of him. When the Land Rover came round the bend Mpole would be standing right in its path, near enough to startle but not near enough to be struck (it seemed he knew about Land Rover brakes). There was a grassy bank on one side of the track, and Sheena decided to wait up there, behind a pile of stones and closer to the bend. If Dad Allen pulled up a little way past her she would be able to sneak towards the Land Rover through the grass, and hear as well as see what happened.

It did not take the Land Rover long to arrive; but by then the sun was low in the sky. They heard the engine as the vehicle climbed the incline towards the bend. It seemed to be going quite fast, as if Dad Allen was trying to make sure he had a beer glass in his hand by the time the sun touched the horizon. The Land

Rover swung round the bend. There was Mpole, standing solid in the middle of the track, his tusks gleaming in the diminished light. He looked bigger than he was.

There was nearly a disaster. Sheena felt the whoosh of the Land Rover's passing in the grass around her, heard the clang as Dad Allen stamped on the brakes. Then there was a shushing, sliding noise. The brakes had locked, the wheels lost their grip in the loose sand of the track, and the Land Rover skidded forward almost in a straight line, directly towards Mpole.

The elephant had no time to move, and if Dad Allen had turned the steering wheel the Land Rover would have simply carried on sliding, but sideways, with an even greater likelihood of hitting Mpole and some likelihood of rolling over as well.

'That wasn't at all what was supposed to happen!' Sheena could already hear what Mpole would say when it was all over, if Mpole was in a fit state to say anything at all.

What did happen was that *Great White* slid all the way up to Mpole and came to a dusty halt with its radiator just touching his tusks, which he had lowered to protect himself. If they *had* both been elephants, a grey one and a white one, it would have looked as if they were engaged in Mtihani wa Buri. One inch more and Mpole's tusks would have gone into the radiator and he would have had another problem with heat. A few more feet and his whole head might have smashed through the windscreen and Dad Allen would then have had a problem with ivory.

Sheena was now too far away from the Land Rover; and Mpole was too close to it. She would have to get closer so that she knew what went on; he would have to back away so that he could do his thing – how can you charge forward when you're already there?

So she crept and he backed. They reached their ideal positions almost simultaneously, he when he was about twenty feet further along the track, she when she was opposite the Land Rover's rear wheels (and still hidden among the grass and rocks, but also still up on the bank so that she could see into the vehicle). *Great White*'s windows were partly wound down ('No such thing as air conditioning when this car was built,' Dad Allen often boasted), so she could also hear every word.

Or she would have been able to, if there had been any. To begin with there was only a stunned silence. Then, eventually, there was a 'Wow!' from Thomas (was that a proper word?) and an undoubted word from Dad Allen (but quite an improper one).

Mpole was standing still, recovering – gradually – from the unexpected. Then he got on with business. He raised his trunk and snorted.

'Sounds more like a horse than an elephant!' Sheena said to herself.

More things were said in the Land Rover.

'Reverse! Reverse!' (Mum Allen).

'Go closer! Go closer!' (Thomas).

'I've dropped Annie!' (Amy).

Amy was sitting on Sheena's side of the rear seat. She had held Amy out of the window to let her see the elephant. Then she had dropped her. Sheena peered through the grass and could see the silly doll doing *its* thing (being floppy) in the sand next to the back wheel.

In the face of the contradictory demands being made on him, Dad Allen did nothing. That was a signal to Mpole to do more.

He raised his trunk, snorted, *and* flapped his ears.

'He's not really very good at this,' Sheena decided.

Then Dad Allen spoke, three times.

'I'm trying!' (to Mum Allen). He was working the gear change lever, and there was much clunking from beneath the Land Rover, but that was all.

'No chance!' (to Thomas, who was leaning forward excitedly as if he could will the Land Rover to roll closer to Mpole).

'Can't do anything about that!' (to Amy, who was shouting and leaning out of the window, reaching down frantically but vainly towards the languishing Annie).

Thomas was enjoying himself.

'Why was the laptop battery flat?' he asked.

No-one answered.

'It had been charged by an elephant.'

Not for the first time he had to chortle at his own joke.

Mpole now tried harder. He raised his trunk, snorted, flapped his ears *and* shook his head violently.

Dad Allen tried harder as well, and the knob of the gear lever came off in his hand. He looked at it, surprised, as if he'd never seen it before.

'Give that to me!' (Mum Allen to Dad Allen). She grabbed it from his hand and tried to screw it back on to the end of the lever.

'Don't worry, I'll rescue her!' (Thomas to Amy, who had given up shouting in favour of shrieking). He pulled her back from the window, crawled over her, and opened the door.

'Don't you dare set foot on the ground!' (Mum Allen over her shoulder to Thomas, as she worked to get the gear lever knob back on).

'Hang onto my legs!' said Thomas to Amy, obedient as always. He wouldn't set foot on the ground; instead he would execute a death-defying lean.

Why? It was only Annie the Unlovely out there in the dust, and Thomas had often said she was a plain nuisance. ('She's not plain at all – she's beautiful!' was Amy's standard, indignant, reply.)

Because a dramatic rescue would allow him to say to Amy, 'You owe me big time!' – and that might be worth a lot at some future date.

That was the plan in his scheming head. The head within which the plan had formed, however, was now dangling upside-down, half-way to the ground; and the legs at the other end of things were not being hung onto very effectively by Amy, who was after all quite small. In a moment the head landed in the sand, followed by the rest of Thomas.

Amy had only one thing to say:

'You've landed on Annie!'

Mum Allen had several things to say.

'Get back in the car this instant!' was the first. There was no time for the others. While she had been trying to screw the knob back on the gear lever, Dad Allen had been struggling with the lever itself, gripping it lower down with both hands. Whatever had jammed suddenly came free, the Land Rover went into reverse gear, Dad Allen's foot slipped off the clutch, and the car jerked backwards several yards then stopped.

That left Thomas sitting alone in the sand, out in front of the stationary vehicle. He had pulled Annie the Unfortunate out from under him, and was now holding the doll in the crook of his arm as if it were his. He would be thankful afterwards that his parents had decided a video camera would be a distraction from the real experience of being on safari, and hadn't brought one. None of this would be recorded for posterity.

But who would have been using a video camera anyway, at such a crucial time?

Amy, probably; and she would have taken great delight in showing the video to Thomas's friends. He would have had to owe *her* big time to stop her.

Mum and Dad Allen were doing other things. Think of the situation as Mum Allen saw it. Her precious son had been hurled from the Land Rover by unseen forces, was lying badly injured in the track ahead of them, and an enormous wild elephant was about to charge forward and trample him flat.

Mpole was about to do no such thing. He was still being gradual, and was only as far as Phase Four. He raised his trunk, snorted, flapped his ears, shook his head violently *and* took two steps forward.

Just two. But that was two steps too many for Mum Allen. She threw open the door of the Land Rover and leapt out to protect

Thomas.

Dad Allen threw open *his* door and leapt out to protect Mum Allen. In his haste he caught his foot under the brake pedal and fell out sideways onto the track, as floppily as Annie had done.

Amy threw open *her* door and leapt out to protect Annie. It wasn't clear whether she felt a need to save her favourite doll from the raging elephant or rescue it from her mad brother.

Sheena could only watch.

As far as Mpole was concerned, Mtihani wa Land Rover was going strangely wrong. This specimen had not behaved at all as it was supposed to. Human beings had suddenly fallen out of it on all sides and were doing various things. The boy who had tumbled out first was waving a miniature human in the air, and the girl who had appeared last was desperately trying to grab it from him. The man was flapping on his back in the sand with his foot still caught up somewhere inside the Land Rover. The woman was marching towards Mpole fiercely.

'Shoo! Shoo!'

That was the best Mum Allen could think of to say. It had once worked with some cows in a field back in England.

Something else was happening at the same time. The Land Rover was beginning to roll backwards. Its engine was still running, but the rolling had nothing to do with engines. It had to do with gravity (they had stopped on a slope, remember) and with the fact that Dad Allen, also in his haste, hadn't put the handbrake on. He himself had acted as a brake as long as his foot was caught; but then he had managed to pull it free…

Great White really did, sometimes, behave as if it had a brain of its own, and it now looked as if it had decided to quit all this kerfuffle and go back to the campsite.

None of the family noticed; but Mpole did, and Sheena did.

Mpole was concerned because although the Land Rover was going away (which was good) he hadn't made it actually turn around first, and he thought he might fail the test on a technicality; and he also wasn't sure what to do about these human beings it had left behind.

Sheena on the other hand was concerned because *Great White* was her means of getting back to her home and her crunchy biscuits, and she knew it shouldn't be wandering off back down the track like this (it *was* wandering a bit, from side to side). Luckily it was moving only slowly, since the slope was gentle and the tyres kept catching in piles of loose sand.

But 'Goodness knows where it'll end up!' Sheena said to herself. Around the bend (if the Land Rover managed to steer itself that far) the track was smoother and became steeper, and there was a sharp drop on one side.

None of the family was looking. Mpole had taken care of that by going into Phase Five – he had raised his trunk, flapped his ears, shaken his head violently, taken two more steps forward, and instead of snorting had trumpeted. It was a real, adult-sounding trumpet which startled even Sheena (and possibly Mpole). He had undoubtedly decided that the Land Rover should take its humans with it when it left.

Sheena jumped down onto the track and raced back to the pile of rocks behind which she had initially hidden, overtaking the Land Rover on the way (and dodging its wheels as it veered from side to side). The rocks had been heaped up quite high, and hadn't looked very secure. She might just be able to stop *Great White* before it either made its escape or met disaster.

When she got to the pile she stayed down on the track and scrabbled away at the bank. The sandy soil under the rocks was already loose. She had to do this very carefully: if she got her timing wrong both *Great White* and *Little Black-and-White* would come to a halt.

She also had to work quickly.

She heard two things at the same time. One was the deep throbbing of the idling Land Rover engine as *Great White* arrived behind her; the other was the rumbling of the rocks above her as they began to spill downwards. She jumped – and nearly jumped under *Great White*'s wheels. The rocks followed her, tumbling down from the bank. The ones at the front rolled under the nearer of the Land Rover's rear wheels. *Great White* stopped with a gentle bump.

Sheena jumped again, up onto the bank and behind what was left of the pile of stones. She couldn't allow herself to be seen!

So far so good. But what was happening back there on the track? As soon as she was certain none of the family had run after the Land Rover, she moved quickly through the grass to where she could see and hear more clearly.

Mpole's last mock charge had had a curious effect. Instead of frightening the family into moving backwards, it seemed to have made them go forwards. Mum Allen had charged down the track past Thomas and towards the elephant. Dad Allen (having struggled to his feet, tripped and fallen and struggled up again) had gone after her.

'No, No!' he was shouting. 'We need to get back in the Land Rover!'

Mum Allen was intent on staying between this large wild animal up ahead and her son lying injured on the ground.

Except that he wasn't lying on the ground and he wasn't injured. Thomas hadn't been hurt at all. He had stood up to keep Annie out of Amy's reach, and he was now backing away from Amy as she jumped and grabbed. She managed to get hold of one of Annie's legs, and hung on. In their struggle they too were moving towards Mpole, as if they didn't know or didn't care.

All in all it seemed that Mpole was failing this little variation on the test. He looked to be at a loss as to what to do next: he was standing still and shaking his head slowly from side to side, and his trunk was drooping. Sheena wished she could help him; but the family were more important.

Then Thomas managed to pull Annie free of Amy's grasp, and it became plain why he wanted the doll. He walked towards Mpole, holding Annie out as if she were a talisman, a magic object used to ward off evil.

'By the power of this sacred and very ugly relic I command you to return whence you came!' he cried. (He'd recently been reading books about wizardry.) 'Pachydervanish!'

Mpole, now desperate to get things moving (backwards), tried some magic of his own. He knew nothing about wizards, or wands, but decided that he needed to supplement his mock attack repertoire. There was a broken branch lying at his feet. He seized it in his trunk, waved it in the air, beat the ground with it (raising lots of dust) then took several quick steps forward, shaking the branch vigorously.

Thomas realised he was probably outmatched in this talisman business, took hold of Annie by her feet, swung her around his head and hurled her towards Mpole. That might not achieve very much, but it was a chance to dispose of Annie the Irritating once and for all, while claiming to be acting in the interests of family safety.

Mum Allen, who had been startled into stillness by Thomas's strange behaviour, now went into action again.

'Take that as well!' she cried, and hurled the gear lever knob at Mpole. She did better than Thomas. Annie the Airborne had just spun in a high loop and landed with a little bounce on the ground, well short of Mpole. The gear lever knob, shiny, round and heavy and very like a black snooker ball, flew in a straight line and hit Mpole with a dull clunk, between the eyes.

That was the signal for the family to flee for *Great White*. The smallest member ignored the signal and tried to run towards the elephant so that she could get her doll back, and Dad Allen had to pick her up and tuck her under his arm, where she struggled and kicked all the way to the Land Rover.

Which was not where they had left it, of course. It was much further back towards the bend in the track.

That didn't matter too much, since Mpole was not chasing them. He was standing looking at the gear lever knob on the ground in front of him. He had the same look of surprise on his face as Dad Allen had had when the knob came off in his hand.

Sheena was relieved to see the family reach the Land Rover, scramble back on board and slam the doors. All Dad Allen had to do now was reverse round the bend, find somewhere to turn the vehicle, and drive back to the campsite. He would just have to do without his Sundowner tonight (however badly he thought he needed it after all of this), and Amy would have to go to bed without Annie.

Sheena would try her best to explain things to Mpole. He deserved an explanation. He was still standing, motionless, looking down at the round black knob as if it was a thought that had struck him.

Things weren't so straightforward, however. Dad Allen got the Land Rover into reverse, despite the knoblessness of the gear lever (about which he would of course complain to Mum Allen later; she would probably include something about handbrakes in her reply). But could he drive backwards? No. Why not? Because there were rocks behind one of the rear wheels.

Did he know that? No. No-one had noticed the rocks, in the rush to get into the vehicle. So he assumed there was still a problem with the gear box, gave up on backwards and drove forwards instead. He decided he would have to drive off to the right of the track (where there was no bank), go in a short circle on the open ground there, and then rejoin the track facing the way they all (with the exception of a very sulky Amy) now badly wanted to go.

The ground on that side was soft. That only became a problem when they had almost reached the bend and were about to come back onto the track. Dad Allen made the mistake of slowing down in order to do that, and the wheels dug in. *Great White* stopped, stuck.

It stopped well and truly. It stayed stopped even when Dad Allen engaged four-wheel drive (which all Land Rover owners love to do: basically that turns the car into a tank). The wheels just dug in further.

Sheena and Mpole had been pleased enough to see all of this happening, up to the point of stick. Mpole (having recovered from being knobbled) felt he had passed the test; and Sheena had thought the Allens were safely on their way back to the campsite. Annie the Unrescued didn't look too happy, lying forlornly as she was doing in the sand; but Sheena had an idea about that.

So they both watched anxiously as Dad Allen revved the engine and made matters worse.

'How far does the Land Rover need to go back, towards where it came from, for me to pass the test?' wondered Mpole. The Mitihani rules were a bit vague on that topic.

'What can I do to help?' wondered Sheena. She felt responsible for the scare the family had had, and she wanted them to get back to the campsite as quickly as possible.

It was now quite dark. As soon as the sun had dropped below the nearby hilltop, all the colour drained from the landscape. Only *Great White* stood out in the gloom. Sheena ran back towards Mpole.

'They're stuck. Can you help?'

Mpole saw straight away what she had in mind; and it was in his interests also to get the Land Rover on its way. He walked quietly up the track, then stepped off it behind *Great White.* Sheena had trotted alongside him, not speaking. She was confident that he knew what was needed.

Dad Allen was still revving the engine and spinning the wheels so that they dug ever deeper into the sandy soil. There were clouds of dust in the air behind the Land Rover, and they and the gathering darkness meant that he could see nothing in his rear-view mirror.

Mpole lowered his head so that his tusks were beneath the rear bumper and his forehead was against the rear door. He leaned forward. His wide feet gave him a firm platform from which to push. They didn't sink into the sand at all: it was if he was wearing great flat-soled shoes. If Thomas had looked out of the back window he would probably have repeated another one of his jokes (after he had got over his surprise):

'Why do ostriches bury their heads in the sand?'

'To look for elephants that have forgotten to wear their sandals.'

Mpole lifted and leaned some more, the engine roared, the wheels spun, the sand flew up...and the Land Rover rose out of the holes it had dug itself down into. It lurched forward, its tyres gripped, and it bumped over the slight ridge onto the track. Dad Allen, fully believing it was his skilful driving that had freed them, revved the engine, triumphantly this time, and drove off down the track to the campsite as fast as he could.

When the roar of the Land Rover had faded into the distance everything suddenly seemed very quiet.

'Thank you,' Sheena said.

'Thank *you*,' replied Mpole. 'It's sometimes good to do a bit more than a test asks you to do.'

'I'm glad you said that,' said Sheena. 'I still need a little more help. It won't take long.'

She took charge. They went back to where Mpole had made his final rush. Annie the Abandoned was lying where she had fallen. The gear lever knob was nearby. Sheena picked the doll up in her teeth, and Mpole lifted them both up onto his head.

The only way the gear lever knob could be transported was in the end of Mpole's trunk. He picked it up delicately. Sheena felt she needed to issue a warning.

'Don't suck that.'

She had seen what happened to the large sweets called bull's eyes when they were sucked.

'It needs to stay the same size otherwise it won't go back on the gear lever.'

They set off into the dusk, Sheena and Annie side by side on Mpole's head and swaying like a pair of tiny Indian elephant mahouts, Mpole trying hard not to suck.

For some reason it was Thomas who was first out of the tents when the sun rose next morning.

'Quick everybody!' he shouted.

'Come and look at this! It's the Gear Lever Knob Fairy!'

Chapter Eight: Tumbusi

Mpole seemed rather troubled next morning. Sheena tried to find out why.

She had done her best to explain the strange behaviour of the people who had variously jumped and fallen out of the Land Rover the evening before, and had told him who the Allens were. Mpole had a strong feeling for the idea of 'family', and that helped him to understand why Sheena had worked so hard to make things turn out all right for the family of which she was a part.

They had turned out all right for him as well, so that wasn't the cause of his unhappiness. He had passed Mtihani wa Land Rover, he was now sure.

Was he moping over the difficulty he had had in deciding what to do in an unexpected situation? He *had* been rather gradual in his response to events; and he had felt foolish, he confessed, when that hard round black thing bounced off his forehead and rolled forward on the ground.

But no, that wasn't it, he also said. He had lived for a long time with the knowledge that he was gradual, so he hadn't learnt anything new about himself the evening before.

'*I* learnt some new things about *you*,' said Sheena.

'You're very fierce when you need to be. You're very helpful when you're asked to be. And you're very strong.'

That all cheered him up, but only briefly.

'Are you not feeling well?' Sheena asked a little later, from the top of his head. They had travelled some distance from the campsite.

Mpole had not said where they were going (he hadn't said much at all) and he had slowed his walk until it was not much more than a rocking movement that barely carried him forward. He was being extremely gradual, in fact. He also stopped frequently to give the dung beetles something to work on – a sign that he was worried. Thomas would have taken the opportunity to try one or two jokes.

'What was the nervous elephant doing on the motorway?'

'About one mile an hour.'

'How often does a nervous elephant go on the motorway?'

'About five piles an hour.'

'Your lion scratches have bled a bit.'

Sheena turned and looked at them again. The mud had cracked and begun to fall from his back, exposing deep and ugly gashes in his skin. Blood was trickling from some of them.

'It's not my back, it's my front that's the problem; or rather it's what's in front of me,' Mpole said.

'I'm really not looking forward to the next test.'

'Tell me what it is.'

Sheena was beginning to be concerned. Mtihani wa Land Rover had sounded easy but had turned out to be tricky for everybody. If the next test sounded tricky it might turn out to be impossible.

After they had propped Annie up against the front of the Land Rover windscreen the night before, in a sitting position with her arms around the gear lever knob in her lap, they had walked down onto the river bed to drink. Sheena had been tempted to stay near Tembo Campsite from then on, and have some mild adventures thereabouts. She was thinking that next morning she might wish Mpole good luck and send him on his way. When they climbed back up onto the bank, however, she found that they were back once more at the spot where she had come up against Swila. This time the snake began to slither out of the darkness in her head; the awful memory of that attack flooded back; she remembered how much she owed Mpole; and she knew she could not leave him to face the remaining tests alone.

As they moved further away from the campsite Sheena felt twinges of boap. She was leaving Amy and Thomas unprotected again. The problem was that she'd sort of given a promise to Mpole as well (just by doing what she'd done so far) – a promise to help him some more with Mitihani Saba. You have to be very careful in this life, she thought, not to make promises that can't work together. Not for the first time she wished she was two cats instead of one.

Now Mpole himself was faltering. Maybe he was about to give up on trying to become Accepted, and there would be no more tests. She couldn't let that happen. What kind of lonely life would he lead then, a Singleton for the rest of his days?

'It's… Mtihani Tembo Pakee – the Test of the Only Elephant.'

Mpole had decided to share his fears.

'Have you ever seen a Mighty Tusker?' he asked.

'*Mighty Tusker*? Don't you mean *big elephant*?'

Sheena knew how words like *mighty* can be used to make things seem larger than they are, in the same way that *just, only* and *all* are used to make them seem smaller.

'Well…er…yes; but the Only Elephant is more than that. Much more.'

He talked on. The Only Elephant lived deep in the

Dimdarong Forest, way down in the Park. It was an area that park visitors were not allowed into. It was an area that even the Park Rangers went nowhere near if they could help it. It was difficult to enter, and there was a good chance that anyone who went in wouldn't get out again. Some major animals lived there.

The Only Elephant was the most major of those, by far. He was very old indeed, and vast in size. His tusks were so long that they almost reached the ground, despite his great height. His memory was flawless. He knew everything that had ever happened to elephants in Baragandiri, to elephants in other parks – and sometimes, it seemed, to elephants everywhere. He had fathered more elephants than all the other current males in the whole Baragandiri Herd put together. He had probably turned around more Land Rovers as well, and even crushed a few.

That all sounded very impressive, Sheena decided as Mpole talked, but nothing much that another elephant should worry about.

Then Mpole explained that the Only Elephant was different from the other animals that lived in the Dimdarong Forest, but not just because he was an elephant, and the only one there. They had all taken refuge in the forest; he, however, had been banished to it.

'He's the Only Elephant not because he lives alone there but because he's the only adult elephant ever to have become Unaccepted. All male elephants are Sent Out from their families, like me, when they begin to grow up. But elephants are never Sent Out from the Big Herd, unless they've done something great and terrible.'

'What did he do?'

'No-one knows. It all happened so long ago that he's also the only one who was alive then who's still alive now. That's another reason why he's called the Only Elephant – he's the only one who knows some of the things he knows.'

Something of a mystery, then. But why was Mpole so afraid of the Only Elephant?

'Because I must face him. And I must answer his questions. And he knows the answers already. He knows everything.'

'If he knows everything why should he want to ask questions? That seems a bit of a waste of time, like tests for the sake of tests.'

'To see if *I* know the answers. To see if I tell the truth. To see if I know my*self*.

'Not just that. He will make me understand what I'm most afraid of. That will be my next test beyond this one – to face my greatest fear.'

Sheena couldn't begin to imagine what Mpole's greatest fear might be. Mice? Elephants were afraid of mice only in cartoons. People? He'd done pretty well when faced with the mixed bunch of the night before – a boy who thought he was a wizard, a woman who threw things, a tiny human being that flew then flopped, a little girl who danced and screamed, and a man who fell down a lot. Snakes? He was more than competent there. So what, then?

Mpole himself didn't seem to know, and was apparently in no hurry to find out. In fact, as he talked about the Only Elephant his pace, already little more than a sway forward, developed almost as much sway back. In other words he virtually stopped. If he went much slower he'd be going backwards, and he'd become the Laudarg Elephant.

'So I may just take a few days off before I go South,' he concluded.

'That's fine. But *I've* only got a few days left before I need to go much *further* South,' said Sheena, and she did a quick calculation. They had arrived in the Park on Saturday. Today was Tuesday. So much had happened!

There was still a lot *to* happen, if Mpole was to get through Mitihani Saba by Sunday. That was when the Allens were intending to pack up and return home. Whether or not she would be able to see Mpole through the remaining tests would depend on what they consisted of – and how quickly he got on with them.

'So you'd better get on with your tests if you want me to be with you when you do them. No *days off*, as you put it. *Off* is something you are not allowed *to* put.'

When Sheena listened to herself talk she sometimes heard Mum Allen's voice in there somewhere. Dad Allen had once said that dog-owners and their dogs grew to look like each other. Could pets and their owners come to sound alike, as well? Frightening thought!

Another thought Sheena found frightening was the idea of someone else knowing everything about you, even things (such as what you were most afraid of) you didn't know about yourself. Sheena was by nature a very private animal; and she also believed she knew herself quite well. But maybe not, maybe not...

Being confronted by the Only Elephant could be a wholly daunting experience. Who knew what you might be forced to face, both within yourself there and then, and in the test that would follow? Fortunately it was Mpole, not Sheena, who had to do the facing. She was committed to helping him, though.

The first thing to do was get him there.

'How far is it to the forest?' Sheena demanded.

'Two days' walk.'

'Well, you'd better walk fast. You've only got one day.'

The idea of a cat bullying an elephant may be disturbing to those (usually big creatures) who believe size should count more than anything else; but Sheena was installed up on Mpole's head like a second brain, and for the moment the dominant one. He could be allowed to do his own thinking and deciding later, when room had been made for such things in the time available.

The journey South was long, and made even longer by the fact that they were travelling West as well – Mpole's idea of South had been rather vague (perhaps another sign of his reluctance to head for Dimdarong). Some time after leaving the area of the campsite they had passed between two conical hills, both of them some distance away. Sheena was sure she recognised them as Getanga Hill (but there was no sign of an eagle in the sky) and Ketabong Hill (but she was too far away to see the Silver Baobab, let alone the warthogs' termite mounds). She told Mpole something of her previous adventures in the neighbourhood. Part of him was obviously very impressed; a larger part of him, however, was obviously thinking about other things.

He walked more quickly than Sheena had thought him capable of; but when his wounds began to bleed again she wondered whether she was doing the right thing in urging him on. It was remarkable how often something that was clearly the right thing to do became less clearly right once you had started doing it.

She had lots of time for such philosophical thoughts as they swayed onwards, sometimes in open savannah, once, for a short while, along a faint dusty track, and sometimes through patchy woodland.

They stopped only once, in mid-afternoon. They had just emerged in a clearing in the middle of the longest stretch of trees so far. Sheena's eye was caught by something gleaming whitely in the long grass to one side of the clearing. Mpole saw it at the same time and changed direction towards it.

It was a scatter of bones, heavy-looking and bleached by the sun. They had been there a long time, it seemed: the grass had grown up around them. There was no skull. There were no tusks either, but Sheena had no doubt these were the remains of an elephant. They were much too big to be anything else.

The tip of Mpole's trunk moved gently over the bones. He wasn't sniffing them as much as touching them, caressing them almost. He picked one up, let it hang in his trunk for a while, then

put it down a few inches away from where it had lain before. He did the same with another one. Then a third. There was no order to this rearrangement that Sheena could see. It wasn't something Mpole was doing to the bones, it seemed to be something he was doing *for* them, as if they needed to be moved every now and again, needed to be handled ('trunkled' came into Sheena's mind), needed to be remembered.

'I remember this elephant,' said Mpole; but his voice wasn't sad. 'I remember him well. He used to make us laugh, when I was very small.'

He stood for a while longer, looking down at the bones. It was clear that he was not upset by them, as he might have been if they had acted as a memento mori. Sheena knew that phrase because the slightly morbid Thomas had a rat skull on his bookcase. 'That's my reminder of death – my memento mori,' he'd said to his friends. He'd got the term, and the idea, from the wizardry books he'd read. He'd got the skull from behind the school canteen. His friends were impressed (by the skull and by the Latin, in unequal amounts).

No, it seemed that the bones were more a reminder of life for Mpole – the life of the cheerful elephant to whom they had belonged and whom he remembered with affection.

Eventually, he moved on. Sheena looked back. The bones still gleamed in the grass, but were soon out of sight.

By evening they had reached an area where the trees were much larger and closer together. Mpole was having difficulty passing between them, and Sheena suspected he was in increasing pain from his wounds. She had to crouch down on his head to avoid some of the low branches, and she could hear some of them scraping roughly along Mpole's back. He shuddered beneath her when they did so.

'We should rest now,' said Mpole. 'It isn't very much further.

'I would like to go off by myself for a while. I'll put you up in a tree if you like.'

'No, down on the ground will do, thanks. I need to find something to eat.'

She didn't wait for Mpole to reach for her with his trunk, but turned and ran along his back (taking care to avoid his scratches) and down into the curve of his tail, from where she could jump sideways to the ground.

She was glad to be down and about, after the long trek. She had her nose among the grass in no time, and was hardly aware of Mpole moving off into the trees. She assumed he wanted to prepare himself for the test the next day, by doing some hard and quiet thinking. It might help him to face the Only Elephant if he had *some* idea beforehand of what his biggest fear might be.

Sheena rooted through the grass, lifted her head, listened, rooted some more. She was hoping to scare something small and scurrying out into the open. Nothing happened. She gradually worked her way between the trees, and before long came to an open space with a single lumpy tree in the middle. She did not pay much attention to the tree until it suddenly rose into the air.

That's what it seemed like to Sheena, who saw it happen only through the stems of grass. The tree's dark shape lifted, flapped over towards her, and settled over her like a great black cloak as, startled, she crouched close to the ground. A blustery wind ruffled her fur.

The tree was still there in the middle of the clearing, however, when she looked again; but it was now a bare tree, with gnarled and empty branches. Around her on the ground were twenty or so very large vultures.

All vultures are very large in comparison with a cat. Some have a wing-span of nine feet. Even if you don't count their wings (and you shouldn't, if you want to be fair to cats, since cats don't have wings, although they sometimes wish they did, like now) they're big. Their bodies in themselves are twice the size of cats', and heavy-looking. Vultures are also very ugly.

Very, very ugly. Very, very, very ugly, Sheena now decided. The heads and necks of these great birds were like sharp question-marks ('What's in it for me?' seemed to be the question), and bald except for some patches of soft, yellow down which seemed out of place, like babies' hair on an old man's head. Their eyes were as cold and beady as Swila's had been. Their bodies were bulky and black, and altogether they looked like ancient, scaly schoolmasters wrapped in dusty academic gowns.

The vultures shuffled into in a perfect circle around Sheena. Then they waddled towards her, making the circle even tighter so that there was no way through. They looked mean, and hungry. They thrust their awful faces at her, and she recoiled.

'Oh, so you think we're ugly!'

The croaky voice came from directly behind Sheena; but when she swung round to face the speaker she could not tell which vulture it was who had made that assumption. They all had their beaks firmly closed, and all were motionless.

'We think we're beautiful.'

The vultures did seem rather proud of themselves – there was a haughty, arrogant air about them.

'You may believe you're the only smart-looking black-and-white creature around, but watch this!'

This voice came from behind Sheena also; but before she had time to turn around the vultures did: with one hop they sprang and spun, all at the same time, so that they were facing outwards and their backs were towards Sheena. At the same time they opened their wings wide. This meant that the wings overlapped, and Sheena found herself fenced in by a solid wall of black and white feathers – black because the vultures were black overall, and white because at the base of each of their bodies there was a large white patch.

'Flap, flip, thump!' and they were facing towards her again. The whole thing looked as if it had been choreographed (planned and practised like a ballet); but the vultures were ballet dancers only of an ageing, overweight variety, dressed in baggy black leotards. They landed back on the ground with heavy thuds, raising clouds of dust any ballerina would have been ashamed of.

'See? We're very elegant.'

This also came from behind Sheena. She jumped round towards the speaker this time, but none of the vultures in that part of the circle showed any sign of having opened its beak. The effect was unsettling. It meant that she didn't know which vulture to talk to, when she eventually found something to say.

'Very nice. I approve. Let me guess: you're white-backed vultures.'

She could speak only to the vulture in front of her; but of course it was one behind who answered.

'Yes we are.'

There was a pause. The vultures were obviously waiting for her to turn around again in the hope of identifying the last speaker. Sheena had realised that they were playing a game with her, so she didn't turn, and she didn't say anything. That forced the vulture behind her to speak once more.

'Don't think we're scavengers, either. We're the MHP.'

'Mean and Hungry Parasites?'

Sheena's growing annoyance at being hemmed in and taunted like this was showing through. She had spoken boldly but perhaps unwisely. The voice of the vulture behind her became even harsher.

'No. The Municipal Hygiene Patrol.'

There was an element of SRS in the comment – Setting the Record Straight. Vultures were often thought of as nasty, dirty birds who sat around in the trees or hung around in the sky waiting to eat dead things. Wildlife programmes usually showed them squabbling over horrible bits of flesh, their eyes red with petty anger, their faces red with blood. In fact, they performed an invaluable function in the wild, clearing away the remains of carcasses before they could decay and spread disease. Sheena knew that, and was prepared to give the birds credit for it; but she wasn't prepared to give them credit for being polite, since they were definitely not. It was rude to turn your back on someone who was talking to you; but it was equally rude to address only *their* back and refuse to speak to them face to face.

'You can give yourselves whatever grand title you like,' Sheena now said to the silent and impassive vulture directly in front of her.

'But the truth is, isn't it, that you eat disgusting scraps of other animals' left-overs?'

This time, as she finished, she sprang round to face the other way. She caught the vulture directly behind her just as he opened his beak to reply, and threw him into confusion.

'Well…er…' was all he could say. Then he closed his beak firmly. Sheena did notice how big, and curved, and strong-looking a beak it was.

'We dine at the King's table.'

The voice came from behind her again. She didn't turn round: she'd had enough of this game. She fixed her gaze on a vulture a little to the right of straight ahead. She would talk only to him from now on, she decided. The others could reply if and how they chose.

'I suppose by *the King* you mean the Lion?' Sheena said.

'But male lions are scavengers too: they're lazy creatures who hardly ever hunt for themselves,' she continued. 'If you dine at the King's table, as you put it, you're eating left-over left-overs. That's like chewing a piece of gum you've found sticking under a chair, when you know that whoever put it there found it sticking under a desk and had a chew of their own in between times.'

She didn't for a moment expect the vultures to understand the comparison, but hoped the general idea was plain. It would do them no harm to puzzle over the details.

'We eat only the finest carrion,' (voice behind).

'Carry on, then,' (Sheena, still looking at the vulture right of straight ahead). 'And you can also carry on and tell me why you've surrounded me like this. *I'm* not carrion.'

Carrion was dead meat.

'We eat only the finest carrion *when we can'* (another voice behind, but not the same one: at least she'd forced them to change their routine a bit).

'When we can't, when we're hungry like now, we eat *what* we can. You may not be carrion, but you're dead meat.'

Then Sheena felt a great peck on her rump. It was very painful. Automatically she jumped round to defend herself. But which vulture had attacked her? None of them was moving.

'Ow!' Another peck, more violent than the first. Another jump round. There was no movement among those vultures either.

Ordinarily, after an attack of that nature, Sheena would have issued a warning: 'The next scrawny bird to peck at me with his horny beak can *ex*peckt to feel the *im*peckt of my teeth and claws…' or some such fighting talk.

She had no way of telling which vulture had pecked her, though, and her warning would have the hollow sound of an empty threat. So she hesitated.

The next attack was even more vicious. She felt the fur being torn from her rump and knew that blood had been drawn. This was not a game, this was life or death. The vultures would slowly rip her to pieces. Even as she swung round to face this latest tormentor she felt another stab and another tear and another trickle of blood.

But at least she knew which bird had struck at her this time: when she jumped round she saw that the vulture right behind her had a tuft of black fur in his beak. So she leapt for him. She leapt for him with teeth and claws at the ready, driven by pain as much as by fear, but also by anger at being treated as no more than a piece of raw flesh.

All the vulture did was straighten his neck so that his head was out of reach, rise up on his legs, open his wings, and batter her backwards with them. She fell, and immediately felt a stab and a rip in one of her rear legs. There was no point in turning this time: she was helpless. The vultures just needed to keep pecking away at her defenceless back half until she could no longer use her legs; then they could waddle in, pin her down with their long claws, and continue to tear.

There was another stab and another piercing pain, and this time the pull on her flesh was so powerful that she was dragged a little way backwards before fur and flesh gave way. Already the vultures were jostling even closer together, eager to get within reach. They would soon be pecking at her head as well.

Then a strange thing happened. There was a thud behind Sheena, a pause, and the vultures to her left started to topple sideways, left to right around the circle, each one as he fell knocking into and pushing over the one next to him. They fell like dominoes, still in their tight ring, with much hissing and squawking as they did so. Sheena turned to follow the ripple of their collapse. When the circle was completed all the vultures were lying instead of standing.

After a moment's shock and stillness they tried to disentangle themselves and struggle up. In vain: for Mpole was walking steadily round on the vultures as if they were a circular pathway, using his trunk to knock over once more those who had half risen.

Only two vultures from the last part of the circle managed to free themselves from the confusion. They took clumsy steps, flapped heavily up into the air, then flew ponderously back to the tree from which they had come. They settled into it with two distinct crashes. They would be back, when Mpole and Sheena had gone.

The rest of the flock had been thoroughly trunkled then trampled. They would never rise into the air again, except in the stomachs of other vultures. Their own days as the Municipal Hygiene Patrol were over.

Chapter Nine: Tembo Pakee

The sky above the trees was bright and clear next morning; but they were now back among large tree-trunks and heavy branches, and there was a grey-green gloominess beneath the thick overhead foliage.

Mpole and Sheena weren't too happy either, Sheena because of what was behind her (her sore rump) and Mpole because of what lay ahead of him that day.

She knew what he must be feeling: it would be something the same as Thomas would feel if he had to face the Headmaster, the Scout Master, the Arch Wizard and his Grandfather all at once – knowing he'd done something very bad but what?

Sheena tried to lighten the mood with an elephant joke of her own modification:

'What goes clump, clump, clump, squelch, clump, clump, clump, squelch?'

'I don't know,' said Mpole, flatly.

'An elephant with a vulture stuck to the bottom of its foot.'

Mpole didn't find that very funny.

'I don't feel good about killing those creatures, you know,' he said.

'Vultures can't help the way they're made. They need to feed, the same as the rest of us. I should just have chased them away.'

Sheena felt chastened for a moment. Then she remembered how much pleasure the vultures had obviously taken in taunting her then pulling her to pieces with their beaks. That wasn't need, it was cruelty.

She felt better, and decided not to remind Mpole about how satisfying he had obviously found it to flatten Swila.

She wondered what other animals would make of the circle of crushed birds – the smashed wings, splintered legs, flattened bodies. No doubt another Municipal Hygiene Patrol would arrive soon to take care of the problem, as part of what was called the cycle of life and death. Would it be possible, if you were a vulture (Sheena pondered), to eat your own parents without realising it? If you did realise what you were doing, would that stop you?

That was grim thinking, and it matched the grimness of their mood as they moved further into the darkness of the trees, which continued to grow in size.

Sheena's hind-quarters ached, although her wounds were not deep. Rather they were stinging patches of raw flesh where the skin and fur had been torn away. She continued to lick them clean, balancing as best she could on Mpole's head as he swayed along, but some were in an awkward position and she couldn't reach them. They would have to take care of themselves.

She was more worried about Mpole's lion-inflicted gashes. ('Some King!' Sheena snorted. That had been a cowardly attack; but at least the lion had been hunting for himself, she conceded.) The wounds were not bleeding now, but an unhealthy-looking yellow crust had formed over them, and her sensitive nose told her that they were not healing properly.

Sheena did not know what to expect when they found the Only Elephant, and Mpole wasn't saying much.

'Have you begun to work out what you're most afraid of?' she had enquired.

'Right now, it's not being able to answer the Only Elephant's questions,' Mpole had replied. 'But there must be something more than that. There always is. And I don't know how I will behave when I have to face it.'

He was plainly afraid of being afraid. Maybe *that* was what his greatest terror was; maybe that was what every Singleton's greatest terror was, and the Only Elephant told them all the same thing when they came to him. Maybe the Only Elephant was just a big fraud, like a fortune telling machine at a fairground which gave everybody who put money into it a card with an identical, vague message: 'Your future will be full of good things and bad things.' What help was that to anybody?

'The only thing we have to fear is fear itself.' Philosophical rhubarb! Fears were much more real things, with teeth and claws – and sometimes beaks – which had to be dealt with, very often by means of your own teeth and claws, and beak if you had one. And trunk and tusks and large feet, if they were the weapons you had been given. And brain, the most effective weapon of all.

That was where Sheena hoped she might be able to help Mpole once more. He had shown himself to be a better thinker than he thought. A brain was like a muscle, too: the more you made it work, the stronger it got. It didn't get bigger like a muscle, however: it couldn't, since it was held inside a hard skull. It got more complicated instead. That meant it could do more complicated things.

'I hope the Only Elephant's questions aren't too complicated,' Mpole said at one point, as they walked on.

'I can give you six bits of advice,' said Sheena as if she was an expert (but she *had* listened to Dad Allen talking to Thomas about how to succeed in exams).

'One: don't try to answer a question until you understand it.

'Two: if you don't understand it at first, think of a different way it could have been asked.

'Three: use your imagination, and turn words and numbers into pictures if you can.

'Four: when you've eliminated all the possible answers except one, accept that that one must be right.

'Five: don't just think about what a question means, think about why it was asked.

'Six: say what sounds right to you, not what you think will sound right to somebody else.'

Mpole's silence suggested he was having difficulty taking all of that in.

'Not surprising,' Sheena had to say to herself. She had just given Mpole a crash course in examination technique.

They had already discussed how to organise things when they found the Only Elephant. Sheena would hide behind Mpole's ear again.

'Think of me as your second brain,' she said, when he began to worry.

She knew she could tuck herself away securely there, and as long as he didn't get in a flap over the questions she would be able to stay out of sight. From that strategic position she would be able to...well, not tell him the answers, but lead his thoughts once more: they had come to a clear decision about that. She hoped the line between leading and telling would be as clear.

After two more hours they were in the heart of the forest. The gloom was intense, the way ahead blocked by an entangled mass of close-together trees and thick creepers. As they moved further in, a silence had fallen around them: the birds had stopped singing, the small animals scurrying, as if to mark their passage. There was an *old* silence about the place they had now reached, however: they knew there had been no sound there before they arrived, had been no sound for a long time.

There was an open space in front of the entanglement – not open to the sky, since the large branches met overhead, but with enough room for Mpole to turn round...which he now did, as if he were going to head back in the opposite direction. He knew he was Close; and Sheena sensed it as well.

She sensed the struggle inside Mpole, too; but he barely paused in his turning, as if retreat had been only a revolving thought, and in a moment he was facing forward again.

It was time for Sheena to disappear. She scrambled down from his head into the angle behind his left ear. She found a good purchase with all four paws in various folds of tough skin, and for a moment clung upright, looking over the top of the ear.

Mpole walked Closer.

Peering into the gloom Sheena began to make out a shape darker than the darkness of the trees. It was behind the screen of creepers. Elephants have poor eyesight, and she knew she was seeing something Mpole probably couldn't.

'There's something there! Oh! He's as big as a tree!'

She was whispering, but the feeling in her words was very loud.

For he *was* as big as a tree, this great creature. She had no doubt this was the Only Elephant. His body was darker than the tree trunks, and wider. The top of his head – and she could now make *out* a head, as her eyes focused beyond the creepers – was on a level with the point where the tree trunks split into branches.

There were other ways in which the Only Elephant was like a tree, in addition to his size.

There was a stillness in him as if he had grown there over hundreds of years, had never moved, had no need to move.

His tusks hung down to the ground like curved buttress roots helping to support the weight of his enormous head.

Sheena could see that his skin was heavily wrinkled and deeply ridged, like tree-bark that has dried, split and cracked through countless seasons of rain and sun and growth.

Finally there was his eye. (His head was slightly turned, so only one was visible.) It was the only bright thing in the darkness. Through the screen of creepers it looked like a plump, black bird with glossy plumage, sitting high in this great tree of an elephant, watching.

Suddenly there was the rumble of thunder. That was strange – the sky had been clear all morning. Then she realised this was no thunder: it was the rumble of the Only Elephant's voice. The broad leaves of the creepers vibrated in response, as if a giant was gently shaking the whole screen.

'So, you've come.'

They were deep, slow words that sounded as if they had come from way down in the earth and travelled up through the Only Elephant's mighty legs and chest before being spoken.

'Yes.'

Even if Mpole's voice had been normal it would have sounded high-pitched by comparison. It wasn't normal, though, it *was* high-pitched, and uncertain.

'Are you ready to answer your questions?'

Sheena noted *your* instead of *my*: this test was for Mpole, specifically. It was *about* Mpole.

'Yes, I think so.'

Mpole was standing very still, but Sheena couldn't tell whether that was because he was calm (which she doubted) or stiff with anxiety (which she feared).

'How many legs do you have?'

What kind of question was that? One designed specifically for a *very* gradual elephant, Sheena thought.

'Four.'

Mpole had answered without hesitation. There was some relief in his voice, but also a touch of pride at having got his first answer right.

'He must be even less sure of himself than I realised, to be so pleased at so little,' Sheena thought now. Then she had a moment's anxiety of her own. *Was* that the right answer, or did the Only Elephant somehow know that Mpole had four more legs behind his ear?

The questions continued.

'How many legs can you stand on without falling over?'

This time Mpole didn't reply immediately. For a moment it seemed that he might lift one leg to try the answer out before he gave it; but then he said, 'Three.'

'How many legs *could* you stand on without falling over?'

Ah, the questions were becoming more subtle.

'Think about what that means before you answer it!' Sheena whispered. She was afraid Mpole would decide it meant, 'How many legs *could* you stand on, if you really *tried*?' He *might* really try, lift two legs, and fall over, which would be embarrassing and could jolt her out onto the ground. As far as she knew only Indian elephants, trained in a circus, could stand on two legs.

'What's the difference between an African elephant and an Indian elephant?'

'About three thousand miles.'

(*'And the size of their piles,'* Thomas might have added.)

'Think about the MHP!' Sheena said.

Mpole thought. There seemed to be no time limit on the test, which was just as well.

He must have eventually remembered the crunch of vultures under his feet.

'I could stand on lots of legs, if they belonged to small creatures I was walking over,' he said.

'Good lateral thinking!' Sheena whispered. Mpole had gone sideways in his mind, and worked out that *legs* didn't have to mean *your legs*.

The Only Elephant was giving no indication that Mpole was answering correctly; but perhaps the fact that the questions kept coming was a good sign.

'How many different combinations of *your* legs could you stand on, if you could only stand on three at a time?'

Mpole seemed to understand *combinations* well enough; but he tried to find the answer the hard way, muttering to himself as he struggled.

'Let's see. My two front legs and one of my back ones. That's one combination. Then my two back legs and one of my front ones. That's two combinations. Then one back leg and one front leg and a different front leg. That's three combinations. Then my three back legs…'

He'd lost his way and would have to start again.

'Think of a different way the question could have been asked!' Sheena whispered urgently.

The pause this time was long. Then Mpole spoke towards the Only Elephant.

'You mean if I wanted to rest each leg in turn, how many times would I have to stand on the other three?'

There was a deep rumble from behind the screen of creepers, but Sheena couldn't tell whether it was of agreement or annoyance. The Only Elephant probably wasn't used to *answering* questions.

'That's easy! Four!' said Mpole.

'Well done!' said Sheena. Instead of whispering this time she spoke quietly against his skull, just behind his ear. She had decided that he would be able to hear and understand the vibrations more easily than he would her whisper.

'You are standing on one leg,' said the Only Elephant.

'No I'm not!' said Mpole.

'Shh!' said Sheena. 'Use your imagination!'

'You are standing on one leg,' repeated the Only Elephant, even more sternly if that were possible.

'You can stand on your front left leg only if you're also standing on your back right leg.

'You can stand on your back left leg only at night.

'You can stand on your front right leg only if your front left leg is off the ground.

'You can never stand on your back right leg during the day.

'Which leg are you standing on?'

This was much harder than the other questions; and it certainly wasn't one Mpole could try out on the ground or that's exactly where he would end up.

'Is it day-time or night-time?' Mpole directed his question towards the screen of creepers.

'Irrelevant!' Sheena said against his skull.

'Irrelevant!' the Only Elephant rumbled.

'Oh!' said Mpole. He had been hoping for a clue. He obviously didn't have one, himself.

Sheena was having a problem as well, with the problem.

'Turn words into pictures,' she said quickly. 'Try drawing it.'

That would be much better than trying to do it.

Mpole stamped each of his heavy feet into the earth in turn, making four deep indentations. Then he stepped off to one side of the diagram he had created, and stood looking down at it. Sheena did her best to look down at it as well, from behind his ear.

'Now eliminate the possibilities,' she said.

He did, slowly, muttering to himself all the while.

'Front left only if standing on back right…so can't stand on front left by itself.'

With the tip of his trunk he drew a line in the dust, through the front left footprint.

'Back left only at night…back right not during the day…so back legs always on ground, or off ground, together.'

He drew a line through both back footprints. That left only the front right.

'Front right!' he announced loudly, before Sheena had had a chance to check his working. But she thought he'd found the right answer. He must have done, for the Only Elephant began to rumble out the next question. She was relieved. Then Mpole got in the way.

'Wait!' he cried. 'Not right!'

He'd obviously carried on thinking. That can be dangerous, sometimes.

'Oh Help!' Sheena thought, 'He's going to change his mind and say *front left*. That's not right.'

No, it wasn't right, it was left, and Sheena herself was getting muddled now. But Mpole meant something different.

'That's not the right answer!' he now exclaimed.

'What about if it was night-time…'

'Irrelevant!' Sheena tried to interrupt him. She was afraid he was about to mess things up even more. He was.

'What about if it was night-time and I was standing on my back left leg? That wouldn't mean I *had* to be standing on my back right leg as well!'

There was another long silence. Then the Only Elephant spoke. For the first time there was something less than Almighty Confidence in his voice.

'Enough thinking questions,' he rumbled. Maybe *he'd* had enough of those. Mpole had done marvellously well.

'Let's see what you *know*.'

There followed lots of questions Sheena found very dull, probably because she knew none of the answers – questions about plant-type food and where to find it, rivers and where they ran, birds and their behaviour (some mild interest for her, there, and she could have added an occasional bit of information).

Then the Only Elephant got personal.

'How many sisters do you have?'

(That sounded like another one of those easy lead-in

questions: Mpole might soon face more complicated stuff, such as:

'How many sisters can you stand on without falling over?'

'You can stand on your oldest sister only at night.'

'You can stand on your youngest sister only when your oldest sister is off the ground.')

'Two,' said Mpole. 'One younger and one older.'

That should make the calculation easier, at least; but the Only Elephant had a different kind of question in mind.

'Did you ever chase them?'

'Yes. We used to run around all the time.'

There was a note of wistfulness in Mpole's voice. This was a life he had left behind.

'What did you feel when you chased them?'

'Excited. My baby sister made me laugh. She was always falling over.'

'And when you chased your older sister?'

'Excited, like I said. When she chased *me*, too, but in a different sort of way. She bullied me sometimes. She's five years older than I am.'

'Were things different towards the end, just before you were Sent Out?'

'Well, they were a bit, I suppose. My older sister stopped chasing me a few months ago. And she tried to stop me chasing her. She said I was becoming a nuisance.'

'How?'

'Well I wouldn't stop. Our mother said I was getting *too* excited – too *grown-up* about it.'

This was becoming more like a cross-examination than a test, Sheena thought. What was the Only Elephant suggesting?

'Think about why he's asking these questions,' she whispered, forgetting to speak against Mpole's skull. There was something here Mpole should be wary of. She risked a peek over the top of Mpole's ear in the hope that the Only Elephant might have shown more of himself; but he had not. He, and his intentions, were well hidden.

'Did you ever chase other young females?' he asked.

Mpole didn't answer straight away. Then, 'No,' he said.

'Why?'

'Well, it was no fun.'

'Why?'

There was another pause. Mpole was struggling with something.

'Remember Number Six. Speak the truth!' That was all Sheena could do to help.

'They used to laugh at me.'

'Why?'

This questioning was relentless. Sheena remembered how frustrated the family got when Amy whyed on and on – 'Why?...Why?...Why?'

'Why are you whying?' Thomas would sing to the tune of 'O Come, All Ye Faithful'. He'd asked his parents for a wireless card for his computer, as a birthday present (the school had a wireless network, and he thought he might be able to skip some lessons and stay in bed if he was able to log-on while he had a lie-in). 'And I'd like a whyless sister as well,' he'd added as an afterthought. He got neither.

The Only Elephant wasn't just whying, however, he was demanding; and Mpole was not frustrated, he was frightened. He was frightened about what he was going to have to face.

'Because they thought I was slow in the brain.'

There, he had faced it, at least in words. Good for him!

The Only Elephant, however, had decided that Mpole should face it some more.

'So what are you most afraid of?'

'Having to chase females, when I'm older. Having to chase females because that's what male elephants do. Having to chase females and show them that I'm not stupid. Having them decide that I *am* stupid, and run away from me and not stop. That will mean I can never be a father.'

It had all come out in a rush, an indication of how this fear had been held tight inside Mpole, so tight that he had hardly known it was there.

There was another long pause before the Only Elephant spoke again. Sheena had the feeling that he was remembering things deep in his massive head, recalling the time when he had been young like Mpole. This was a life he had left behind, many, many years ago.

'Here, then, is your next test. You must persuade a young cow elephant that you are not stupid. You must chase her and you must get her to stop and wait for you. She must let you come close to her and touch her with your trunk.

'That is all. There will be more, much more, when you are truly grown. But you will have shown, in the meanwhile, that when you *do* become fully grown you will be able to have calves of your own. You will have passed Mtihani wa Mtamba, the Test of the Young Cow.

'Remember, it is a very dangerous test. The Matriarch will be angry. The adult males may try to kill you. Worst of all you may fail. You may find that you will never be a father. That will be very sad for you.'

Suddenly there was movement behind the screen of creepers. The great tree that was the Only Elephant had taken a step forward. The creepers shook as his head pushed against them. The large, glistening eye was close to a gap in the leaves, and was watching Mpole closely. It was fringed with very long, curved eyelashes, and there was a gentleness in it Sheena hadn't expected to see.

Then, unexpectedly, the Only Elephant stepped through the dense foliage, brushing it aside effortlessly, and partly emerged between the nearest tree trunks, so that he could be seen clearly for the first time.

Mpole backed away as if he was afraid of being trampled. Sheena almost ducked back down again but decided that moving would be worse than staying still. She would have to rely on the Only Elephant's poor eyesight – all the poorer, surely, because of his age.

In full view, the Only Elephant was all she had expected him to be – terrifying and wonderful at the same time. He spoke, and Sheena felt the ground tremble again, its vibrations coming up through Mpole's body.

'Your mother is Nusu Pembe, Broken-Tip.'

It was a statement, not a question.

'Yes. She broke the end of one tusk when a tree fell on my older sister and my mother lifted it off. She wouldn't wait for the big males to come and help.'

'I know the story.'

Sheena, once more, detected something happening in the enormous head, beyond social niceties. Parts of a long past were being relived in his memory, she suspected. She began to get a sense of what it must be like to be so thoroughly alone, at the end of a life which must have been so thoroughly full as the Only Elephant's. It was not surprising that he would take this opportunity to reach out, just a little.

The Only Elephant asked no more questions. All he did was give some advice.

'You can go now. The sooner you do Mtihani wa Mtamba the

better. Try not to be too afraid. The only thing you need to fear…' (for an awful moment Sheena thought he was going to finish, '…is fear itself' and she knew she would splutter behind Mpole's ear) '...is not being a father. Then the line that runs through you will stop, and the things that make you special will die when you die.'

Mpole had been dismissed. He had the good sense to fold his ear back against his skull as he turned away. Sheena was well hidden from the gaze of the great eye above. But the Only Elephant spoke after them as they reached the far edge of the clearing.

'You did very well with the questions. The only answer you got wrong was the first one.'

Chapter Ten: Katika Ziwa Salangani

'No, he can't be my father. He's much too old. He was banished before my mother was even born.'

Sheena had tried to explain her feeling that the Only Elephant wasn't *only* the Only Elephant.

'He seemed to know a lot about you.'

'That's his job.'

'*Job*? I thought you said he'd been banished from the herd. You can't banish somebody and then make them work for you.

'He knew who your mother was. He also gave you all those thinking problems to solve, as if he already knew you needed to show that you aren't slow.

'You aren't, by the way. If you were ever slow you've gradually got faster. You'll have no trouble passing Mtihani wa Mtamba.

'That's another thing. He knew what your greatest fear was even before he got you to tell him.'

Mention of Mtihani wa Mtamba made Mpole go very quiet.

'I'm not ready for that yet. I need to plan.'

By *plan* Sheena suspected he meant *put off*, once more. The incidents he had been forced to recall, when young females mocked him, had clearly been very painful, and he did not want them repeated. He now seemed to be punishing himself by thinking about them, as if they had all been his fault.

'He's beating himself with a memory stick,' Sheena said to herself.

She did agree, though, that they should turn their attention to other things before they proceeded to Mtihani wa Mtamba. The raw patches on her rump were weeping yellowish fluid, particularly the ones she hadn't been able to reach with her tongue – the ones she had to twist her head a long way round (as now) to even see. By the look of things she would have to find a way of treating them. By the smell of things the wounds on Mpole's back needed some drastic healing as well.

'You're in no fit state to go courting anyway,' she said.

'Your back's a mess. Do you know any elephant medicine that might help? Plants and things?'

'Not really. I would need to ask. There's no-one I *can* ask, right now.

'There is one thing we could try, though. Lake Salangani.'

He explained that Lake Salangani was in the north-western part of the Park. It was a soda lake. That meant nothing much could live in it. It also meant it was very good for cleaning open wounds, particularly when they had begun to fester.

'The water burns, but it also cleans,' Mpole said.

'You just have to take care not to stay in too long, or it begins to cause blisters.'

'Sounds like fun,' said Sheena.

It was, in an unexpected way. They had left Dimdarong from the same point they had entered at. They turned away from the route that would have taken them back towards Tembo Campsite, and walked Northwards for the rest of the day (or rather Mpole walked and Sheena dozed on his head. All that brain work had tired her, so more precisely she dozed, slipped, grabbed, stayed awake for a while, then dozed, slipped…)

It was evening by the time they reached the shores of Lake

Salangani. The dark, calm water stretched as far as Sheena could see, even from the top of Mpole's head, and the other side of the lake was lost in a twilight haze.

Mpole did not hesitate. He waded straight into the water, which was shallow for a long way. As he disturbed the lake a harsh, metallic smell arose, as if water had boiled away in the bottom of an aluminium pan. Then the lake water rose higher and higher up his legs and Sheena began to get anxious.

'Er...I'm not really a swimmer, you know.'

What she meant was, 'I'm a sinker.' She hadn't recovered yet from her experience in the mud pool, where she had suddenly found herself under and going down.

'Couldn't you just do your trunk trick, and spray me?'

'No, you need to soak in the water for a while so that the soda can do its job. Don't worry, I'll keep you safe.'

Soon, as he continued to wade away from the shore, the water was up to his shoulders, then it was washing onto his back as far as his wounds. He gave a little trumpeting squeal and Sheena wasn't sure what it signified. She suspected it meant, 'Ouch!'

She herself was still high and dry on Mpole's head. How was this going to work for her?

She soon found out. He continued to wade, and the water continued to rise, up and over his head. It lapped at her body, and she stood. It climbed up her legs and she moved forward to Mpole's trunk, which was raised. She started to climb. She soon looked like a shipwrecked sailor, shinning up the only coconut tree on the island as the tide came in.

Then there was a great sucking noise from Mpole's trunk, and his rounded body surfaced, like a submarine rising from the waves.

How had he done that? She had assumed he was walking

along the bottom of the lake. Maybe the lake was getting shallower again.

He rose until his mouth was clear of the water and he could speak.

'No, no, no! Come down from there! You need to go right into the water. Just sit still on my head and let me do the rest.'

'But the water won't reach me. The lake's too shallow here.'

She was secretly relieved. She was frightened of the water, and a bit frightened of the ouch. She hoped he wouldn't be able to find the deep bit again.

'No it isn't. I'm swimming.'

Swimming? Surely elephants were too heavy to swim?

There was a whoosh of air from Mpole's trunk and he sank again. Then Sheena remembered Archimedes.

Archimedes was a fish, a very large grouper Thomas had adopted in the Caribbean. He lived at the Fish Farm, just along the road from their apartment on the seashore. He was about four feet long, and the oldest fish at the farm. He had a pool to himself. He had become something of a local celebrity, which is why he would never be turned into fillets.

Archimedes was not his fish farm name, it was the name Thomas gave him after Dad Allen explained how (like most fish in the sea) he helped himself to rise and sink in the water by using his swim bladder. He filled it with air when he wanted to swim near the surface, and let air out of it when he wanted to go deeper.

Dad Allen's explanation had been a bit more complicated than that (he was very keen for his son to understand such things). A Greek called Archimedes had worked out how an object floats in water. It floats by pushing water down and out of the way ('displacing' it was the word Dad Allen used). The displaced water pushes back with equal force and stops the object sinking further. That helped Thomas to understand why boats could be made out of concrete, even though he didn't altogether understand what his father said was Archimedes' Principle:

'An object immersed in a liquid will suffer an upthrust equal to the weight of water it displaces.'

So Thomas gave the big fish the name Archimedes. He spent a fair bit of time at the Fish Farm, watching Archimedes and occasionally scattering food on the water for him. Then one day when he was swimming in the sea with Amy he tried the Principle out for himself. He found that his body did indeed rise in the water when he took a deep breath and held it, and sank when he let the breath out.

'Look, Amy!' he had said. 'I'm behaving according to Archimedes' Principle!'

Amy behaved according to Amy's Principle – which if she had known a few more big words she would have expressed as follows:

'An older sibling who is showing off should suffer a showing up equal to the amount of silliness he displays.'

She pushed a wave of water into Thomas's face, he took a mouthful, sank out of sight, and came up spluttering.

Now Mpole too was behaving according to Archimedes' Principle, Sheena understood. By sucking air in through his trunk he had made his body bigger without making it heavier. It displaced more water, so he 'suffered an upthrust' (sounded very painful) and floated to the surface. The whoosh had been him letting air out of his lungs so that his body got smaller, displaced less water, suffered less of an upthrust, and sank again.

He sank too far for Sheena's liking. She suddenly wasn't on his head any more: it had dropped away below her. She struggled, but the water came up over her head and down she went into the darkness. The soda stung the bare patches on her rump, but she hardly noticed the pain through the panic. She reached upwards to where she thought the surface must be; but it was too far, too far.

Then she felt Mpole's solid head like a platform under her paws. She dug her claws into its rough skin.

'I'd like to suffer an upthrust now, please!' she said, but she could say it only in her head, since she was submerged.

She couldn't hear anything, but she felt the intake of air through the front of Mpole's head, where his trunk began. It was as if he knew what she had said: he surfaced once more, and as he did so his head came more fully up under her and lifted her clear of the water.

'Oh, sorry!' he said when he heard Sheena gasping.

'Don't you know how to float? Just take a deep breath and hold it.'

Mpole obviously understood Archimedes' Principle without knowing its name (he would probably have thought the Ancient Greeks were some kind of old vegetable, not worth even a sniff).

He didn't wait to see if Sheena was going to follow his suggestion. There was another 'Whoosh!' and down he went again.

Just in time Sheena drew in a large breath, and held it in instead of panting in fear as she had done the first time. She found she was floating quite high in the water, and only had to paddle gently with her paws so that she didn't tip over. She tried letting out a little air, and sank slightly, but not enough to take her head right under. She breathed in again, rose again. She felt in control. She practised a few times.

She knew that if she breathed all the way out she would go all the way under; how then would she be able to breathe in when she wanted to come back up? By pushing down with her paws, of course, so that she could lift her head just a little way clear of the surface. She tried it. It worked. Not only that: she realised that as she pawed the water (she wouldn't have been pleased to know she was doing a dog-paddle) she moved forward.

So Sheena learned to swim.

'I can swim! I can swim!' she cried. There was no-one to hear her. Mpole was sill underwater, with just his trunk showing. So she swam around for a while, enjoying this new ability she had, this new freedom.

'Time to go!'

Mpole had sucked in and surfaced. He had to look around for Sheena, who by now was several yards away, paddling around happily in spite of the stinging of her wounds.

'I think the soda will have worked by now. We'll know tomorrow,' said Mpole.

They were a long way from shore, so Sheena paddled over and climbed up onto his head. He swam for a while, then when his feet touched bottom he walked into the shallows and up onto the flat, grassy edge of the lake.

They found some long overdue food (Mpole a few bunches of leaves at the top of a small tree, Sheena a fat lizard) and prepared to rest for the night. Before she settled down Sheena went back down to the lake and looked out over the black water.

The moon was full, and the ripples on the surface gleamed silver. For a very brief moment she was tempted to walk in and swim some more. The darkness of the water made her change her mind. Maybe nothing *could* live in the soda water; but maybe something could. So she turned back to where Mpole was standing in the moonlight. She had a surprise.

The soda crystals had dried on his skin. They formed a sparkling crust all over his body. What she saw in front of her was not a dull grey elephant but an enormous silver Christmas tree ornament, glittering with moonlight frost.

Chapter Eleven: Mtihani wa Mtamba

The soda had crystallised on Sheena's fur, too. The first thing they did next morning was find a pool of fresh water and hose down. Mpole did the hosing for both of them and Sheena did the spluttering.

'How do you tell the difference between an elephant and a Christmas tree ornament?'

Sheena had realised during the night how much she was missing Thomas and his jokes.

'When you drop an elephant, it doesn't go tinkle.'

It was too early to tell whether the soda water of Lake Salangani had done to their wounds what they hoped it would. Mpole wanted to find the herd, however, so they left the lake and began to move Eastward, back in the general direction of Tembo Campsite.

Mpole was intensely worried by Mtihani wa Mtamba. Sheena knew that *pachyderm*, the scientific name for an elephant, meant *thick-skinned animal.* Mpole didn't seem to be one, at least as far as the herd's young cows were concerned. They seemed to have hurt him, lots, in the weeks and months before he was Sent Out.

'They used to call me *Ukungu*,' he said. 'It means fog.'

The edges of the lake had been hidden in a thick mist as the sun rose.

'Why *Ukungu*?'

'They said it was because I was dense, and wet.'

Mpole smelt better: his wounds had lost their yellow crust and were now just dark brown gouges in his skin. Sheena wondered if the scars of battle might make him more attractive to the young elephant cows.

He seemed to know exactly where the herd was.

'I can hear things you can't,' he explained.

'Elephants make a deep rumbling noise that can be heard a long way away. Listen.'

He should have said, 'Feel.' Sheena heard nothing. She had expected him to raise his trunk, and trumpet. Instead she felt powerful vibrations in the skull on which she was sitting. They resonated up through her whole body, and she imagined sound waves radiating out over the trees.

The only other time he had done anything like that was when he was approaching the Accepted Ones in preparation for Mtihani wa Buri. She had thought then that nervousness was making his tummy rumble, and out of politeness she had said nothing. Now he raised the pitch a little and she could hear as well as feel the signal, a sort of heavy trundling.

'When an adult elephant makes a noise like that, it carries many miles,' Mpole said.

They crossed much open ground during the course of the morning, and eventually reached the Ubi River. It was not dry here, but had almost stopped running. There were nevertheless some surprisingly deep-looking pools in the river-bed. Sheena wanted to get off and swim, but Mpole wanted to move on. So they did what Sheena wanted (she was very good at getting her own way, and that was only partly because she had learnt some tricks from Amy). She splashed and swam while Mpole foraged for food. Then he had to wait while *she* found something to eat.

They crossed the river and continued East into what seemed

to be a large loop in the river bed. Before long they saw the herd in the distance. The next step for Mpole was to find a young female, preferably by herself.

Sheena thought she might be able to help him focus on his task by telling a Thomas joke.

'How does a male elephant find a female elephant lying down in the long grass?'

There was only silence from Mpole.

'Very attractive.'

That didn't make him laugh; but it seemed to make him stop. Then Sheena realised he had stopped because he had, right then, found a female elephant lying down in the long grass.

The rest of the herd was still quite a long way away, partly screened by a grove of trees. There were twenty or so elephants of different sizes, intent on tearing up grass tufts and placing them delicately in their mouths. This particular elephant had obviously eaten enough and had decided to lie down for a rest, and the others had moved on. Lying down during the day was quite an unusual thing for an elephant to do; but this turned out to be quite an unusual elephant.

As they approached she scrambled to her feet and turned towards them.

'You shouldn't be here,' she said.

'I came with *him*,' Sheena said. Then she realised the young cow was talking to Mpole.

'I'm talking *to* him,' the female elephant said. 'He shouldn't be here. He's been Sent Out. He's only allowed to Come Back when he's much bigger.'

'But I'm *getting* bigger,' Mpole said, 'gradually.'

'What are you doing here?'.

'I came with *her*,' said Mpole, and his trunk curled up towards his forehead and pointed at Sheena.

That wasn't a very good start, Sheena thought, if he wanted to win the young cow over with his boldness. Sheena didn't know what a female elephant might look for in a potential mate, but she didn't think timidity would be a part of it. Mpole was trying to hide behind a cat – a difficult thing for an elephant to do.

'What *is* that talking bump on your head?' asked the young cow.

'Er…a brain…I mean a brat…I mean a cat.'

Mpole was very flustered. Sheena had the feeling that right now he would swap where he was for the bottom of the mud pool. Maybe it had something to do with the cow elephant's eyelashes, which were very long.

'She's a miniature big cat. She asked me to show her an elephant herd. There aren't any where she comes from.'

He was making this up.

'Ooh, you fibber,' Sheena thought to herself; but a part of her was pleased at his inventiveness. She looked to see if his trunk had grown any longer.

'I told her I'd bring her here so that she could see for herself how a family can be run by females, with no males around. She's interested in things like that.'

Sheena looked down to see if his trunk was trailing on the ground yet. If so, might he step on it and fall over? That would be even less impressive than his timidity.

Mpole was talking about her as if she was one of those feminists Thomas had had to learn about in History – women who fight for female power. ('I'm not a feminist, I'm a felinist!' she would tell Mpole indignantly, later. 'I don't believe in females being in charge. I think cats should be in charge!')

Mpole continued addressing the other elephant. At least he

hadn't run out of words yet.

'She'll be very impressed by what a good job you and the Matriarch do between you,' continued Mpole.

This was beginning to sound like what Thomas would call Chatting Up. It was something he was just beginning to show an interest in, while pretending to scorn it.

'Why are you chatting me up?' said the young cow. She obviously wasn't a gradual elephant: she was being very immediate.

'Er…well…it's what I'm supposed to do,' said Mpole.

Thomas's First Rule of Chatting Up: *Never admit you're chatting up.*

'The Matriarch will be very angry if she finds out you're here.'

'Er…' said Mpole.

Thomas's Second Rule of Chatting Up: *Never say Er.*

'I think you're here to cause trouble. I'll go and tell her.'

Sheena detected what she might have called something roguish in the young cow's big brown eye; but she knew that rogue elephants are male, so she decided it was *naughtyish* instead: the young cow was naughtily – and playfully, perhaps – trying to frighten Mpole.

Playfully, *perhaps*; but the elephant now turned away and began walking towards the rest of the herd.

'Er…excuse me,' Mpole called after her.

The young cow turned back.

'What?'

Her tone was cold.

'Er…You're wrong.'

Thomas's Third Rule of Chatting Up: *The girl you're chatting up is always right.* Mpole was breaking all the rules.

'What do you mean, I'm wrong!' This time her tone was

cryogenic (cold enough to deep-freeze Mpole and preserve him in his half-grown state for years to come).

'I'm not here to cause trouble. I'm here to take Mtihani wa Mtamba.'

'So I'm right. Mtihani wa Mtamba *is* trouble.'

Thomas's Fourth Rule of Chatting Up: *When the girl you're chatting up is wrong, Rule Number Three applies.*

'You young males think you can just come here and practise on us, as if we're part of a game you play. You can easily cause problems for us.

'For one thing we have our reputation to protect.

'For another we have the adult bull elephants to think about.'

Sheena considered only briefly what a bull elephant would look like before she realised that *bull* just meant *male.*

'They can get very ratty if we encourage juveniles.'

Sheena spent rather longer imagining what a ratty elephant would look like. Would it have a tail twice as long as its trunk, and enormous whiskers?

'Why don't you ask her what her name is?' She spoke to Mpole out of the corner of her mouth. He was obviously short of ideas.

'What's your name?' Mpole said.

'You know what my name is, you dumbo. We've lived in the same herd since you were born. I thought that was twelve years ago, but you're talking like a five-year-old. I'm Straight-Tusk. Don't tell me you didn't remember *that*!'

'Tell her you didn't recognise her because she's so Grown-Up now.' Sheena spoke sideways again.

'I didn't recognise you because you're so Grown-Up now,' said Mpole.

'Never mind *Grown*-Up. That's just *Chat*-up,' said the young cow.

Oh dear! Mpole was having a very rough time of it.

'But you don't look the same. Your tusks are curved now.'

That was all Mpole's own work; and it seemed *to* work. There was a short silence.

'Do you think so?' asked Straight-Tusk.

'Yes. They're *very* curved. What have you done to them?'

'Well, I did try ripping off the bark of baobab trees with my tusks, then chewing it. That's supposed to help.'

'You should say thank you to whoever told you to do that. It worked.'

Thomas's Fifth Rule of Chatting Up: *Tell her something she likes to hear. Then tell her again.* Mpole was learning fast.

'You've obviously been barking up the right tree.'

Thomas's Sixth Rule of Chatting Up: *Be witty.* Sheena had doubts about how well Mpole was doing on that score.

'Was it your mother who told you what to do?'

Seventh Rule: *Keep the conversation going.*

'Have you forgotten that as well?' (She didn't call him dumbo this time, Sheena noted.) 'I have no mother. She was killed by poachers soon after I was born. I was brought up by the allomothers.'

''Allo, muther!' was something Dad Allen said to Mum Allen in a broad Yorkshire accent when he wanted to joke in an affectionate way about her northern upbringing. But an allomother was also, Sheena knew, a young female elephant who helped bring up baby elephants. Allomothers were like elephant nannies.

'I've lost my mother too,' said Mpole.

Sheena had noticed that a couple of times he had looked wistfully over towards the grazing herd, as if he wanted to go over and join them. Was he hoping for a quick nuzzle from his mother?

Eighth Rule: *Don't be pathetic.*

'Don't be pathetic!' said Straight-Tusk.

'You haven't lost her. She's still there. You had to grow up, that's all, and leave home.

'Are you really finding life so difficult on your own? Why? I sometimes think it would be great to be Sent Out. I don't like being Kept In. Everybody watches you so closely, particularly when you become old enough to have calves.

'I'm big enough for that now, and it scares me. You've seen what those adult males are like when they go on musth.'

In female elephant talk, *musth* was short for *Male Uppity Syndrome Tee Hee.* It happened to adult males every now and again, when their hormones (he-mones, Thomas called them, ignoring the fact that there might also be she-mones) made them want to run around and climb up on females. They usually looked a bit silly when they were in musth, hence the *Tee Hee.*

'Things can't be that bad for you. You'll be Accepted soon; and in the meanwhile you seem to have found a friend, even if she is an odd one.'

Sheena wasn't very pleased to be acknowledged quite like that.

'Isn't it time you did some chasing?' she asked Mpole, sideways.

Mpole was thinking the same thing.

'I'll only get Accepted when I've passed Mtihani Saba,' he said to Straight-Tusk. 'You're just Mtihani Sita. So here goes.'

He made a sudden movement towards the other elephant. She was taken by surprise, started back, turned, and broke into a run. The chase was on.

But Sheena was off. As Mpole started forward she lost her

grip and fell from his head. She had to twist in mid-air and do something of a backwards flip in order to ensure that she landed well away from his rear feet.

All she could do now was jump up onto a fallen tree-trunk and watch as the next part of Mtihani wa Mtamba unfolded.

Straight-Tusk was quick for an elephant. Perhaps she'd been rehearsing, in her head, ways of eluding the musth bulls. Maybe she'd even been in training. She had developed a technique of changing both direction and speed that made things very difficult for a pursuer.

This particular pursuer, Mpole, was as gradual as he had ever been in working out what she was going to do next. So he kept over-running her and floundering. Twice he nearly fell over.

All the while, as she ran, Straight-Tusk kept her head turned so that she could see what was happening behind her. That gave her an advantage over Mpole who, it seemed, couldn't even see what was happening in front of him. It was almost as if Straight-Tusk was enjoying the game. It was doubtful whether Mpole was.

So they turned and twisted, started and stopped, for what seemed a long time. Sheena did notice that Straight-Tusk was all the time moving further and further away from the herd and towards another grove of trees. Sheena was forced to trot after the trotting pair.

Once they were beyond these trees it seemed that Straight-Tusk got tired of the game. She stopped suddenly.

Thomas's Ninth Rule of Chatting Up: *The boy chases the girl until she catches him.*

Mpole had not expected her to stop, couldn't stop himself, and ran straight into her. He did, however, seem to know what to do next. He lifted his trunk and laid it flat along her back. He probably thought that meant, 'Got you!' but according to Rule

Number Nine it really meant, 'You've got me!'

By the time Sheena reached them they were standing side-by-side with their trunks intertwined. 'Look, they're holding trunks!' Amy would have said. 'Yuk!' Thomas would have replied.

Then they did something even stranger. They put the tips of their tongues in each other's mouths.

'Look, they're kissing!' (Amy).

'Maxyuk!' (Thomas. He had once explained kissing as a way of getting a boy so close to a girl that he couldn't see what was wrong with her.)

It looked as if Mpole had passed the test. Then the test

suddenly moved into a new and more dangerous phase.

From behind the trees stalked an enormous bull elephant. He was partly in musth – he was Male and Uppity; but there was nothing Tee Hee about him. Dark, angry-looking stains ran down his cheeks from glands behind and above each eye. He was shaking his head violently from side to side, which made his ears slap loudly against his head and neck. His great tusks were aimed threateningly at Mpole.

He was nowhere near as big as the Only Elephant, but he was big enough for the job. The job seemed to be to do damage to Mpole.

'You'd better run!' said Straight-Tusk. Thomas's Tenth and Final Rule of Chatting Up was the same as his Third Rule: *The girl you're chatting up is always right.* Mpole ran.

It's more accurate to say that he first of all scattered, which for a single elephant is quite an achievement; but the bull was terrifying. When he got himself back together again and all of him was pointing in the same direction, *then* he ran.

He couldn't out-run an elephant as big as this one. Sheena watched in horror as the great bull broke into a heavy, thumping trot, and very quickly began to gain on Mpole. Straight-Tusk followed much more slowly, as if she didn't want to be there when the big elephant caught up with Mpole.

Mpole had none of Straight-Tusk's swerving and jinking tricks, and could only watch over his shoulder with a wild and frightened eye as destruction bore down on him. There was a sound of thunder as the bull elephant increased speed and came almost within tusk-thrusting distance.

Was it thunder from his large pounding feet? It seemed to be a deeper thunder, as if it came from down in the ground and then filled the heavens, a rumbling of the whole of creation.

Sheena knew in her bones, since that is where she felt it, where this rumbling was coming from. The three elephants, chaser, chased and follower, knew also. They all stopped short, in clouds of dust.

This rumbling could only be from the Only Elephant. He was the only elephant who could shake the world in this way. And the world, the world of Mtihani wa Mtamba, the world of musth and desire and jealousy and fear and anger, came to a halt. This great noise was a reminder that there were more important things than all of those feelings and needs. It told these elephants that they must turn away.

They did. The bull turned away from Mpole and walked off into the long grass as if it was resuming a journey that had barely been interrupted. Mpole turned away from Straight-Tusk as if he had never entwined trunks with her. Straight-Tusk moved quietly off towards the distant trees where the rest of the herd still grazed.

For the moment Sheena was left alone. Now she knew why the Only Elephant was so important to the Herd.

Chapter Twelve: Tumbiri

The Only Elephant was important to the herd because he embodied its spirit. Its deepest history and its most powerful values lived in him. Yes, the Matriarch of each family group or small herd carried much practical knowledge, and enforced many rules. But the Only Elephant *was* the herd, the Big Herd, the Baragandiri Herd.

Perhaps that was really why he had been banished, so that the Idea of the Herd could live in isolation, untouched by day-to-day troubles except when he chose to reach out and change what was happening.

Why would he interfere here? Mpole had only been doing what he was supposed to do; and so had the bull elephant. It was the bull's job (even though it seemed as if he had been driven by no more than jealous rage) to ensure that the females were preserved for the strongest and fittest males, and kept away from youngsters who had not yet proved themselves. That was how the strength of the herd was maintained, even if it sometimes meant that individual elephants had to face punishment or death. So why had the Only Elephant got in the way?

Mpole tried to understand, and Sheena tried to help him, as they moved away from the other elephants. They had almost given up when Sheena remembered something the Only Elephant had said.

'What was that about the line that runs through you, and the things that make you special? Maybe it's because he *knows* you're special that he saved you. Maybe the Herd needs the line that runs through you to continue. And maybe one day you'll do something really important.'

Mpole said nothing. He was a long way from seeing himself as a hero. He was still struggling to see himself as normal. He might return to the herd one day, and maybe find Straight-Tusk again, but not for a long time. He must now turn his back on her, and on his family, for years to come.

'I'd like to visit *my* family now, please,' said Sheena.

It was the next morning. Sheena calculated that it was Friday. There was one more test to do. It sounded easy. It would take them the rest of the day, however, and she needed to check that the Allens hadn't changed their travel plans, which had been to leave Baragandiri on Sunday. She and Mpole were not far from Tembo Campsite. She would just drop in and sneak around for a little while, long enough to see what the family were up to, then she and Mpole could resume their journey.

The journey would take them out of the Park. Elephants sometimes went beyond its boundaries, for a variety of reasons. That caused trouble. Sometimes they strayed onto the roads that ran nearby. They could be hit by cars and trucks, and injured. It didn't do the cars and trucks much good either.

'How can you tell when a car has run into an elephant?'

'Its trunk is at the front.'

It also caused trouble when they went close to the local villages. Life was hard for the people there: the soil was poor, and the rains could fail, so they sometimes had trouble feeding themselves, and they often had trouble growing enough to sell. The villagers were far from happy when in addition a clump of elephants came stamping through their crops, eating the best of them and trampling the rest.

'How does an elephant eat maize when he's sitting at his computer?'

'By cereal intoface.'

All Mpole had to do to pass the test was eat some water melons. He would thereby prove that he could get to a human settlement – in this case Kinga Village – and that he was not overly frightened by all the noise and fuss the villagers would surely make if they found him there. Not much hard thinking in that, hardly any danger, and a luscious meal in the middle. Not much hard thinking because Mpole just needed to follow the track to get to the village. Not much danger because elephants were protected, even when they were outside the Park, and the villagers were not allowed to harm them. Finding a way into the sweet flesh of the large, firm water melons might be the hardest thing Mpole had to do.

The Land Rover was not at the campsite. Sheena was disappointed. Monkeys were. Sheena was outraged.

They were everywhere. Up in the trees, of course. On the ground, scuttling around the cooking area looking for scraps (there weren't any: Mum Allen kept a very clean kitchen).

Three or four youngsters were jumping up and down on one of the tents, playing what looked like King of the Trampoline. The idea was simple: bounce all the other monkeys off. Even worse, the bumps and jerks shaking the wall of the other tent showed that there were monkeys inside that one.

Sheena knew immediately what kind of monkeys they were. Vervets. The males were unmistakeable. What Thomas would have called their monkey nuts were a bright green colour, or a bright blue, or something in between. The other something in between was bright red. Quite a colourful display, all in all.

All in all Sheena thought the vervets shouldn't be there.

'Take me into the middle of the campsite,' Sheena told Mpole. 'I have some things I need to say.'

She had dealt with monkeys before, but big ones – baboons – with enormous canine teeth. These much smaller ones should not present too much of a problem. A little lecture from her and they would be off.

Mpole took up a position between the two tents. Sheena stood up, on his head.

'Excuse me!' she called out loudly. 'Can I please have your attention?

'I think you should go now. Fun's over.'

'Fun's just beginning!'

The reply came from overhead. So did a hard little custard apple. The tree was full of unripe fruit. The monkeys must have come here in the hope that it would be ready to eat. Having failed to find anything edible in the tree, they were now trying to find it on the ground...and in the cool-box...and in the pots and pans...and in the tents.

The custard apple bounced off Sheena's head. It had been thrown very accurately by a small male monkey above her. He threw another one, and it struck Mpole just over the eye. The monkey obviously fancied himself as a custard apple pitcher. There was a danger that the other monkeys in the tree would join in: they were watching closely, and there was lots of ammunition.

The monkeys foraging on the ground, however, and the ones jumping up and down on the tent, paid no attention.

Not so with the ones in the other tent. They seemed to have got in by unzipping the tent flap, and three or four now came tumbling out to see what was happening. The first one had an armful of tangerine oranges. Those behind were carrying an assortment of things – a packet of soup, a bottle of ketchup, a large onion, and Annie.

Mum Allen, for once, hadn't done too well. It was very unwise to leave foodstuff in a safari tent. It seemed Amy hadn't done too well either, in leaving her doll behind: Annie was now being dragged along in the dust by one leg.

Sheena had turned to look at these new troublemakers. 'Thwack!' Another custard apple hit her on the back of the head. She was thankful the Allens hadn't chosen to camp under a sausage tree.

She very sensibly took up her behind-the-ear position and Mpole very kindly folded the earflap back against his neck so that she was largely protected from the missiles, with only her head showing. She carried on making her speech from this much less commanding position.

'The lease to this campsite is held by the Allen Family of the International School of Ubango. I am their designated representative. I hereby give you notice that you must vacate the property immediately or face the legal consequences.'

'Thwack!' another custard apple on the back of her head. More monkeys were arming themselves, picking the hard fruit and moving onto branches closer to Sheena and Mpole.

The monkey dragging Annie the Unhappy in the dust reared up on his hind legs and stalked towards Mpole. Annie's head bounced along the ground behind him. The custard apples stopped flying; but they still threatened to fly.

'And you'd better put that down right now. If its owner comes back and finds you treating it like that you'll be in big trouble.'

Sheena had run out of legalistic language, and in any case had decided that a less formal approach might work better. These monkeys were a rag-tag bunch, Pirates of the Tree-tops, always on the move, always ready to attack or run, raiding when they could, carrying off what they couldn't eat on the spot. They weren't the sort to be intimidated by big words.

The monkey who had brought the bottle of ketchup out of the tent had tried unsuccessfully to open it, and now deliberately dropped it on a rock so that it smashed. He began to lick up the contents.

The one who had walked towards them on his hind legs stopped in front of Mpole, still holding Annie by one foot, and looked boldly up towards Sheena. He seemed to be the leader of the troop.

'Why do you want a doll anyway?' Sheena asked him. 'It's only a child's toy.'

'We need a decoy, an imitation one of us. We're having some trouble with an eagle and we want to deal with it. We have to have something that looks like a monkey but isn't one. This will do.'

Looks like a monkey! Amy would have been incensed to hear that. Thomas would have been delighted.

Sheena herself had had some trouble with an eagle when she was last in the Park. In fact she had had a lot of trouble. But she didn't think she should approve of the use of Annie to sort out the monkeys' problems.

'Tell me how you'll use her,' she said. She thought that maybe talking about Annie as if she was a person might encourage the monkey to show the doll some respect.

The monkey didn't oblige.

'We're going to use it as bait,' he said.

'We're going to prop it up out in the open and hide in the grass nearby. Then when the eagle swoops we're going to jump on him and make sure his swooping days are over.'

'Why can't you just use a real monkey? What about that one up there with the custard apple in his hand? He looks very useable, very expendable.'

Sheena was all for getting your own back when you can.

'That's the whole point. No monkeys are expendable, as you put it. We value all the members of our troop. We've already lost too many to the eagle. It must stop.

'In any case our instincts are too strong. Not even the bravest among us would be able to stop himself running when he saw the shadow of wings on the ground.

'We'll use this floppy little human being. It doesn't seem to have any instincts. Unless, of course, you'd like to help instead.'

'Oh...er...*I've* got instincts. Very strong ones,' Sheena wasted no time in saying.

Her instinct was to stay as far away from eagle talons as she could. She remembered all too well how powerful they were.

She couldn't just abandon Annie, however. She knew how upset Amy would be if she got back to the campsite and found her beloved doll gone. Almost as upset as Thomas would be when he realised the bottle of ketchup was no more.

A lot of chittering now went on among the monkeys. The ones in the trees came down (a final custard apple just missed Sheena) and the whole troop began to move away from the campsite.

'Follow them!' Sheena told Mpole, and he started to.

'Where do you think you're going?' asked the troop leader, turning back towards them. He was still dragging Annie in the dust.

'I might be able to help you,' said Sheena.

'I've got very good eyesight. I could be your spotter: I could tell you when the eagle is coming.'

'The trouble is you're spott*ed*,' said the monkey.

'You're black-and-white spotted. The eagle will see you.'

'Won't that help?' said Sheena.

'The eagle will see me easily. It will come to investigate, and when it swoops down on the bait you'll be able to jump on it all you want.'

'But won't that make *you* the bait?'

'No, that'll still be this floppy little human being, as you called it – her name's Annie by the way. I'll be down in the hole by then.'

'What hole?'

'The hole in the ground you're going to find. The hole in the ground near the long grass you'll be hiding in. I'll have drawn the eagle's attention to Annie and it will dive on her instead of me, then you'll be able to dive on *it*.'

That was the best plan she could think of, to stay both close to Annie and safe. Once the uproar started she could grab Annie and make off with her. The monkeys and the eagle could fight it out without her help.

After much noisy arguing among the monkeys, and a few punches – it seemed to be a democratic little society, this – the plan was agreed on.

The monkeys knew all the holes roundabout, and chose one at the edge of a clearing. It was at the base of what had been a termite mound before it collapsed into a pile of ochre-coloured, sandy soil.

The monkey leader stuck Annie up on top of the partly flattened mound. Sheena settled down close to her, also up high and in the open. Mpole had been sent away. He seemed happy to go – none of this interested him very much.

The attack group of monkeys disappeared into the long grass

nearby. They would have to stay very still, which is not an easy thing for monkeys to do. Sheena would have to stay alert, which is not an easy thing for cats to do after a busy morning. She wanted a nap; but the thought of eagle talons got in the way of that. So she and Annie sat and looked at each other.

For a long time. Then some more. Sheena drifted a little.

When it all happened, it happened very quickly. A shadow came between Sheena and the sun, and she suddenly felt cold; but it was an inner coldness, not a coldness of flesh and fur. She had not been watching! The eagle was upon her!

But not quite here, not quite with its talons in her, yet. Without looking up (what need was there to look up?) she sprang into the dark tunnel.

Then she sprang out again. There were teeth and eyes in there! She didn't take the time to find out exactly how big, but they were big enough. At least the eagle didn't have teeth, so she would take her chances in the open air.

Her timing (even if it wasn't altogether hers) could not have been better. The eagle had aimed for her, and had dropped towards her with its talons outstretched ready to grab what looked like a plump meal. Then the plump meal had suddenly disappeared down a hole. The eagle checked in its fall, swerved away, rose slightly on its broad wings, but then turned and swooped on the other creature on the mound, which seemed as if it might be edible also. It sank its talons into the second meal just as the first one popped out of the hole again. What *was* going on?

The monkeys had been waiting for Sheena's warning, and had been trying all the while to keep their heads down and stay still. But Sheena had not given a warning. She had given a frightened, uncatlike squeak as she dived into the hole, and a frightened, uncatlike squawk as she jumped out again.

The only monkey to react to those strange sounds was the custard-apple-thrower. He was a useful catcher as well as pitcher: he leapt out of the grass and grabbed the eagle near one of its wing-tips just as it seized Annie in its talons. At the same time Sheena's jump took her out of the hole and onto one of Annie's legs.

She would claim afterwards, when she told Mpole the story, that this was an act of bravery, part of her rescue mission. In fact she dug her claws into Annie's leg, and held on, by instinct rather than design.

So the episode acquired a kind of symmetry. The eagle came

down, Sheena came up, and Custard Apple came in, all at once. Then began a three-way tug of war, with the cat trying to pull the doll down onto the mound, the monkey trying to pull the eagle sideways into the grass, and the eagle trying to pull everybody up into the air.

On the basis of strength versus weight, the eagle would have won. Its wings were enormous and powerful, and beat with a great waft and whoosh that began to lift Custard Apple, and Annie, and Sheena, off the ground. But Sheena's back claws dug into a tangle of fine grass roots which criss-crossed the pile of earth, and the fact that the monkey was holding on right at the tip of the eagle's wing meant that the great bird was unbalanced and began to twist around in a circle. It had to let go of Annie.

Sheena fell back onto the ground with Annie on top of her. The eagle became airborne and beat its way heavily towards the nearby trees, with the monkey still clinging to the end of its wing. The great bird of prey was tipped to one side and pulled to the left by the monkey's weight, and it could not clear even the first tree it came to. It landed with a smash in the upper branches, with Custard Apple still attached.

The grass around the mound erupted in a swarm of monkeys running towards the tree. They would need to get up into it before the eagle broke free, or before it got its beak and talons into Custard Apple.

Sheena was very quick to withdraw her claws from Annie's leg ('Sorry!' she said), pick the doll up in her teeth, and jump down from the termite mound into the grass. There was a crashing and smashing sound in the tree as the monkeys sorted out their problem. Sheena just ran.

She never did find out what had been hiding in the hole.

Chapter Thirteen: Mtihani wa Matangomaji

Annie was not in very good shape. There were puncture holes in her shoulder where the eagle's talons had gripped. Her left leg partially hung off where Sheena had hung on. All Sheena could do was lean her up against the custard apple tree and hope that Amy wouldn't be too upset.

Thomas made things worse.

The Allens arrived back not very long afterwards. Sheena was up in the tree, waiting. The Land Rover roared into the campsite and stopped, sharply and with a bit of sliding and slewing, in a cloud of dust (Dad Allen liked to think he would make a good Tembo Trophy driver). The dust drifted towards the tents, and some of it went in through the open tent flap. When the family saw that happening, they jumped out of the Land Rover in a hurry. They immediately found the signs of an animal raid scattered around in the grass. Dad Allen crawled into the tent to see what damage had been done. Mum Allen followed him: she knew it would be her job to clear the damage up, whatever it was. Amy went in after them to get Annie.

Thomas, however, had seen Annie propped up against the tree. He also found, near her, what he regarded as his ketchup bottle, broken and with a pool of ketchup alongside. On the principle that nobody should suffer alone, he picked up the intact bottom half of the bottle and poured its contents over Annie. Then he hid the pieces of broken glass behind the tree-trunk.

'Amy! Amy! Come quick! Annie's been murdered!' he shouted.

When all of that had been sorted out, and the Allens had decided the campsite had been visited by monkeys rather than overrun by lions (and Amy had accepted that her suspicions about Thomas's part in things would just have to be harboured for the moment), Sheena left. She had found out what she needed to know.

'It's a good job we're only here for two more days,' Thomas had said. 'At least I'll be able to have ketchup when we get home on Sunday.'

'No you won't,' said Mum Allen. 'That *was* the ketchup.'

'Yes I will,' said Thomas. 'That wasn't the ketchup I've got in my homework drawer.'

The only thing Thomas never had in his homework drawer was homework.

Sheena hadn't arranged to meet Mpole anywhere in particular; but she was sure he would know where she was, and find her. Elephants seemed to know things, a lot. She hadn't walked far from the campsite when there was a rustling up ahead and the back leg of an elephant came out of the foliage. Mpole was in reverse.

'How do you get an elephant into a small space?'

'Select the elephant and click on Insert.'

'What command do you give an elephant when you change your mind about having it in the small space?'

'Back-up.'

Now Mpole was backing-up out of a small space, a clearing among the trees in which he had been browsing.

'Hello,' he said.

'I thought you'd be along soon. Did you manage to help the

monkeys?'

'Not really, but I managed to help Annie. She's back at the campsite safe and unsound.'

She told Mpole what had happened, approximately.

'Clever! Plucky!' said Mpole. But he was talking about the monkeys. Then he started talking about the Test of the Water Melons. Sheena felt herself to be a bit unacknowledged for what she had done, a bit let down. Then she felt herself to be a bit picked up, as Mpole curled his trunk around her and lifted her onto his head.

'Time to get on with the test!' he said, quite cheerfully.

Perhaps his eagerness to take this test had something to do with the rumbling in his stomach, which Sheena was sure had nothing to do with communication. Elephants liked water melons.

'What is it when an elephant eats 2.2 pounds of water melon?'

'A kilobyte.'

'What is it when an elephant eats 22 pounds of water melon?'

'A megabyte.'

'What is it when an elephant eats 220 pounds of water melon?'

'A gigantibyte.'

They walked roughly North-West from the campsite, crossed the river bed twice, and after a longish while passed, in the distance and away to their right, a group of buildings that Sheena decided could only be Baragandiri Lodge. Beyond that they went over two tracks and eventually came to what Mpole said was the Park boundary, although Sheena did not know how he could tell that – there were no fences, and no signs.

They climbed up onto open grassland; and before long they could see, ahead of them, the grass roofs of round huts among a scattering of bushes.

There was no need for them to go right into the village. The water melon plantation was between them and the settlement. There were no people to be seen thereabouts. It was a Friday afternoon. Many of the villagers would probably be Muslim, and Friday was their day of prayer. Sheena had noticed that things seemed to slow down for non-Muslims also, on Friday afternoons.

There was another reason why the plantation was empty. The end of the water melon season was near, and most of the crop had been harvested. It would not be true, however, to say that Mpole was about to have slim pickings. His pickings – the few remaining water melons – were fat, and a dark glossy green. Sheena knew they would be very heavy, and difficult for Mpole to pick up in his trunk, since they were also very smooth.

Sheena decided that while he tried to do that, the safest place for her would be on top of his head. She remembered the story Kenge the hissy monitor lizard had told her about how he had once come very close to being crushed by water melons.

Staying up on Mpole's head also allowed her to keep watch for villagers creeping up on them. She knew they were likely to do nothing worse than bang pots and pans together to chase Mpole away; but she was afraid that if he got scared and started to run she might be bounced off his head and left behind.

Maybe breaking into the fruit *was* going to be the hardest part of the test, however. Mpole had several attempts at picking up one of the smaller water melons, but even when he at last succeeded, and brought it close to his mouth, he couldn't manoeuvre it in, and it slipped sideways from his trunk, fell to the ground with a thud and rolled away.

Perhaps a little help from her was needed, or they might be here a long time. If Mpole couldn't put a whole water melon into his mouth, perhaps she could put part of a thought into his head.

'Why don't you take this one step at time?' she asked.
'Oh…alright.'
Mpole clearly didn't know what she meant.
'Put your best foot forward.'
'That would be my left foot.'
As if to remind himself which foot that was, he lifted it in the

air and set it down a little in front of him. A little in front of him was a water melon, much bigger than the one he had tried and failed to eat. His great foot stepped on it, solidly.

The water melon burst apart. It was like a flower opening on the ground. The inside was a deep reddish-pink, and glistened with moisture. Small black seeds were suspended in the translucent flesh. Sheena was not a fruit-eater, but she suddenly felt thirsty.

'Maybe they should really be called mouth-water-melons,' she thought.

By the time she had thought it Mpole had his trunk well into the fruit and was slurping away happily. Then he began to pick out succulent pieces with his trunk's delicate tip, and put them in his mouth. Juice dribbled down his chin. If elephants can smile, he was smiling.

Sheena became a little concerned in case melons fermented like bananas. When that happened to bananas they produced alcohol, and elephants had been known to get drunk on them and go both wobbly and dangerous.

'Why could the elephant who had got drunk on bananas not find his way back to his computer?'

'He kept going offline.'

Instead of stamping on the next water melon, Mpole kicked it – just as effectively.

Sheena felt it was now safe to jump to the ground. She tried a little slurp of water melon herself. The fruit was cool and, mysteriously, neither sweet nor not-sweet. She slurped enough to quench her thirst, then slurped some more because she quite liked the taste; then she wandered off while Mpole ate on.

There was a grove of palm trees a little way past the water melon patch, and Sheena decided she would like to lie in the shade for a while, lick her lips and wash her face free of juice. When she'd done all of that she dropped into a doze.

She awoke to hear human voices nearby. There were three men, and they were arguing.

They had not seen her, but they had seen Mpole. From the sound of it he was still stamping and slurping. The three men, however, did not seem to be annoyed at the sight. These must not be their water melons.

'Yes.'

'No. If we do they will find the carcass soon, and come looking for us.'

'But its tusks are quite big. They must weigh three or four kilos. That's a million shillings.'

Shillings were local money. Shillings were not worth a great deal in dollars or pounds, but a million of them was a lot to a man here – enough to buy a small house.

'They will come looking for us straight away. They will know we have gone into the Park. The elephant we are after is much, much bigger than this one. His tusks are worth twenty times more. We can only shoot one elephant. It must be the big one.'

Then Sheena saw that one of the men had a gun.

Thomas would have recognised it as an AK47. Dad Allen would have known it as a gun that had probably been smuggled in from a nearby country where such weapons had been used in rebellions and wars for many years, and where they were cheap to buy. Mum Allen would have been very angry to find ivory poachers here.

'I'd like to poach *them*,' she had said of such men when she had been reading about the murder of elephants for their tusks. It wasn't clear whether she meant she'd like to shoot them or crack them into a pan of hot water, put the lid on and cook them slowly.

The man who had spoken last seemed to be the leader. His opinion obviously carried the weight of an actual decision, and the men turned away from the melon plantation. The leader set the seal on what he had said: 'We need to get on our way soon anyway, if we want to reach Dimdarong before dawn. The track is very bad in places.'

The three of them walked through to the other side of the trees, and Sheena noticed a battered pick-up truck standing on the track that led to the village. The tail-gate was down and she could see a pile of dirty tarpaulins and, on top of them, a rope and an axe. Gun, axe, rope, tarpaulins – Shoot, chop, haul, cover – Shoot an elephant, chop out its tusks, haul them to the pickup, cover them up…then drive over the country's border to where poaching was more common, and hiding ivory on a ship bound for the Far East much easier.

Shoot an elephant. Which elephant? A very large elephant. A very Only elephant.

The pick-up started noisily and drove off in a cloud of dust and black smoke. Sheena raced back towards Mpole. He had eaten all the growing water melons and had found a large pile that had been picked and thrown aside as much too ripe. He had now moved on from kicking and stamping, and a long way on from slurping gently or picking delicately. He had his head buried in the pile, up to his ears and beyond, and he was making a disgusting noise. So he did not hear Sheena as she burst through the undergrowth. He didn't hear her, either, when she ran up close and called to him.

'What do you call an elephant with a melon in each ear?'

'Anything you like – he can't hear you.'

Sheena made her presence known by jumping up onto Mpole's head, taking care not to slip off into the pile of melons and get slurped. No doubt his eyes were full of water melon as well.

'What do you do if you're eaten by an elephant?'

'Run around inside until you're pooped.'

Sheena didn't want to have to test that piece of advice from one of Thomas's jokes. Mpole recognised the thud as she landed on his head, however, and raised it. Juice streamed down his face, dripped to the ground and began to form a puddle in the dust.

'Washermatter?' he said, spluttering and dripping. For a moment Sheena was afraid the over-ripe melons had indeed fermented, and Mpole's brain with them.

'Okay, you've passed the test. Let's go.'

'But I haven't finished.'

He quickly found he *had* finished.

They moved away from the plantation and the village. Sheena was relieved to find that Mpole was keeping to a straight line. As they walked she told him in more detail what she had seen and heard.

'Can we get there in time to warn the Only Elephant?' she asked. She knew that she was also, in asking that, making a further promise to Mpole – to help, once more.

'No, not all the way. But if I can get close enough to the herd as we travel I'll be able to call to them and they can pass the message on. It all depends where they are, and whether there are other elephants between them and the Dimdarong Forest. We must go quickly.'

Quickly for an elephant was not very quickly. Mpole did his best, but there was no point in running. Elephants have difficulty doing that, and they can't do it for very long. If he got tired and had to stop then the race would be lost. The herd was their only hope, the Only Elephant's only hope.

Chapter Fourteen: Rafiki wa Zamani

The herd was too far away. They had travelled for several hours before the sun went down and for several hours after that, Mpole pacing himself so that he could walk the rest of the night if need be. There was no problem with seeing, since the moon, when it rose, was full and bright, but there was a problem with how big the Park was. They were trying to cover most of its length in too short a time; and Mpole, by stopping and listening intently, discovered that the herd had moved further off to the East and were outside the range of even his biggest rumble. He could hear them, but they could not hear him.

'If only I were older, and bigger!' he said.

'What should you use to send an important message?'

'As large an elefont as possible.'

'Older and bigger aren't available,' said Sheena.

'How about smarter? That's always worth a try.'

'A smarter elephant would find a way to make his rumbles louder so that they could be heard,' said Mpole.

'That was a start: follow that track!' said Sheena. She meant the track in Mpole's thinking, but he was already moving towards a different one.

'*This* track takes us close to Getanga Hill.'

Mpole waved his trunk towards a track that led off to the left from the one they were on.

'I went there once to practise my trumpeting. I found a

clearing set into the side of the hill. I thought that would be a good, private place. I was slow to learn how to trumpet, and I had the idea that nobody would be able to hear me, there, when I made mistakes.'

Thomas had tried to learn the trumpet so that he could play in the school orchestra. The sounds he produced were so bad that he had to practise in the generator house at the bottom of the garden. Then they got so awful that he was allowed to practise only when the generator was running and the noise was horrible anyway. Dad Allen told him, one day, to put a sock in it. Thomas took that too literally, and complained that his sock made the trumpet taste bad.

'You should have used a clean sock,' said Dad Allen.

'Don't have any,' said Thomas.

Everyone knew about Thomas's socks.

The last straw was when Annie the Outrageous appeared at the generator room window one afternoon (held up, of course, by Amy). Amy's favourite doll was wearing Thomas's favourite headphones, obviously as protection against the noise. Thomas gave up the trumpet.

'But there was a high rock face behind the clearing, and the trumpeting came out louder, as if it was bouncing off the rock. When I got back to the herd they all laughed at me. They knew what I had been doing, and had heard how bad it was.

'Maybe I could bounce my rumbles off the rock as well. We wouldn't have to go far out of our way to get there.'

He had no trouble remembering the way.

'Why do elephants never forget?'

'They have lots of RAM (Really Amazing Memory).'

They found the place, found the rock face. It wasn't flat, it curved around like one side of an enormous stone basin, dark blue in the moonlight. Mpole turned his back to it (it faced East, towards where he thought the herd were) and began his rumbling. Sheena could only just hear it, but the cliff face seemed to reverberate and some small rocks came tumbling down behind them. Sheena looked around anxiously in case Mpole's rumbling had started a landslide.

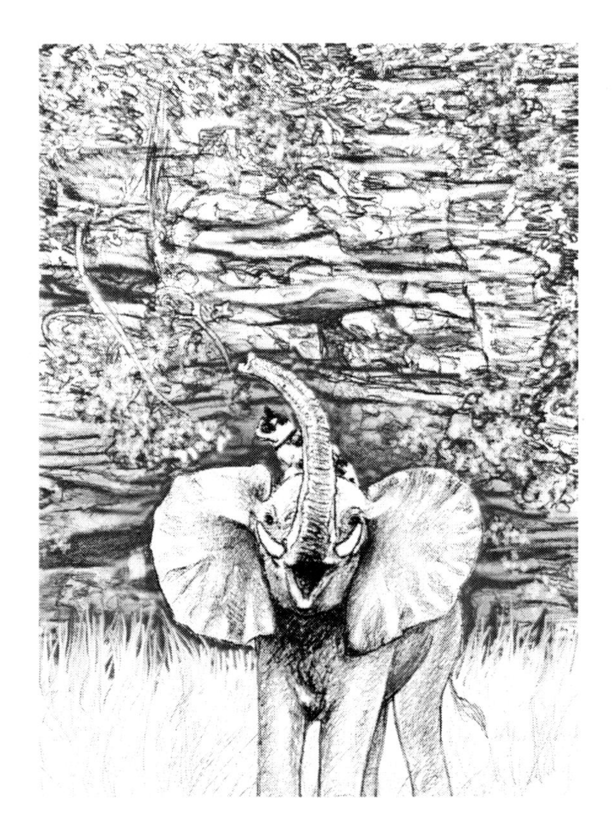

Mpole tried a loud trumpet for good measure, and the sound flew out over the trees into the moonlit sky as if driven from behind by a strong gust of wind. It partly was: in straining hard to trumpet forwards Mpole trumpeted backwards as well, and the two blasts mingled and soared. The sound they produced together was almost musical.

'What do you call a rock group consisting of fat elephants?'

'A broadband.'

He could not know if any of the three calls had been heard. The herd was too far away now for him to pick up *their* rumbles – which was not a good sign. He and Sheena would just have to hope, and continue.

They came down from Getanga Hill to the South and set off towards Dimdarong once more. Mpole was still trying to walk fast, but at the same time trying not to walk so fast that he tired.

Then they had a piece of great luck. There was a tall, ghostly shape standing under a tree. As they got closer the shape became sharper. It was a giraffe.

'Hello-o-o,' it said in a drawn-out, friendly manner. 'What are you doing back in Baragandiri?'

Sheena couldn't believe it. It was Twiga!

Sheena had met Twiga when she came to Baragandiri the first time. The giraffe had carried her South when she was looking for the Lost Allens, had carried her South swiftly on long, loping legs.

'I'll tell you while we're travelling. I need to use the Giraffe Express again.'

She explained what was happening.

'Can you help us?'

Elephants and giraffes have little to do with each other. Giraffes cannot harm elephants, and elephants are no threat to giraffes. Poachers sometimes are, however.

'Glad to. Karibu.'

Karibu was Kiswahili for 'Welcome to my house!' or in this case 'Welcome to my head!' Twiga bent his long neck so that his large head came level with Mpole's. Sheena stepped carefully between the two, and settled down between the furry horns above Twiga's eyes. It seemed a long time since she had last been

there. Then Twiga lifted his head and Sheena was suddenly looking down on Mpole from almost three times his height.

'Right, then,' she said. She experienced a secret sense of power as she issued directions to the two animals, both so much larger than she was. She felt a bit like a general on his horse, deploying his troops.

'Mpole. We don't know that your message reached the herd. Your job is to follow us to Dimdarong as quickly as you can. I don't know what you'll need to do when you get there, but it'll probably be something dangerous. This is going to be the Test of the Big Elephant, and I don't mean the Only Elephant, I mean you.'

'Twiga. You need to get me to the Forest as fast as possible. We have to warn the Only Elephant.

'We must also do something to slow the poachers down.

'Let's go!'

Chapter Fifteen: Akili Kali

Twiga and Sheena soon left Mpole behind. Twiga ran Southwards across the open plain with a smooth, rocking gracefulness which made it seem to Sheena that she was flying, in comparison with the slow wallow of Mpole's deep-sea sort of progress. She might reach the Dimdarong Forest in time after all.

The night was so bright that the giraffe could run powerfully with no fear that he would put his foot in a hole and fall. Their journey through the moonlight was indeed like a flight, but not on wings, more as if on an undulating magic carpet over a flat, shining sea. The faint landscape slipped silently past on either side. Tall grey-blue shapes – trees, other giraffes maybe – drifted by, floating on the broad silver current. Shorter, darker shapes floundered away left and right as if Twiga, skimming across the water's gleaming surface, were driving a path through them.

He seemed tireless, and ran for hour after hour. They talked a little to begin with, before Twiga fell silent to save his breath for running. Sheena was quick to check that the young giraffe who had been attacked by the leopard was still alive: she thought she had seen him as she left Baragandiri that last time, but wasn't sure.

'Oh, yes,' said Twiga. 'But his coat will always be marked where the leopard's claws dug through it; and he's still too nervous to go off by himself.'

This business of going off by yourself or staying with the herd seemed to be a big issue in the wild, at least for some animals. Sheena wondered, not for the first time, what it would be like to belong to a herd of cats.

When the moon eventually sank out of sight and the landscape lost its brightness, Twiga had to slow somewhat, but not by much – his large eyes allowed him to see well in the dark. Once or twice, though, Sheena, whose night vision was even better than his, was able to warn him about things looming up ahead. Not long after that the horizon to their left began to lighten. By then they had reached the first trees of the Forest.

There was no sign of the poachers, no sign of a track even. Sheena had not noticed a track when she came here with Mpole. Maybe it wound in from a different direction. Maybe it stopped short of the forest and the poachers would have to travel the last part on foot. That would be good.

Twiga had to slow to a walk as they began to move through the trees. He seemed to know which part of the Forest they might find the Only Elephant in. Sheena was nervous as they penetrated deep into the gloom. It was like stepping back into night, just when day was coming. Now she was the one who would have to face the Only Elephant, and she did not relish the thought of being looked into the way Mpole had been.

But would they be able to find the great creature? They could walk for another two hours, reach the clearing where he had been last time (if they could even find *that*), and discover that he wasn't there.

'Wait. Wait here, Twiga' she said. 'I need to think.'

Now that the exhilaration of her night-time flight was over and she was faced with the simplest of questions – 'What to do now?' – she hesitated. She hadn't been doing too much thinking recently, other than in a strictly practical way. She had not asked herself why she had become involved in this difficult situation.

After all, it wasn't one of the Mitihani Saba, the Seven Tests she had agreed to help Mpole with. In two days she intended to be back home, getting in the Allen family's way as they unpacked the Land Rover and making it plain that she was not pleased to see them back because she had been so displeased that they had gone away in the first place. Why was she heading blindly into what she would normally call a Problem Area and walk away from nonchalantly as if she hadn't even noticed it was there?

She was hardly doing it for Mpole. Her plan, such as it was, would bring him into great danger. The poachers, if they didn't find the Only Elephant but came across Mpole instead, would surely shoot him (since bigger and older *weren't* available). They might even shoot him as well as the Only Elephant.

She could not be doing it for herself. Yes, she had enjoyed playing the general, and the magic carpet ride had been magical; but a black-and-white cat sitting on a giraffe's head might prove an irresistible target to a man with a gun, and AK47s were wicked weapons.

Then there was Twiga to consider. AK47s were also indiscriminate weapons. Sheena remembered the awful damage the leopard's claws had done to the young giraffe's beautiful coat. The thought of bullets tearing into Twiga was just too terrible.

'Maybe we shouldn't go any further into the Forest,' Sheena found herself saying to Twiga.

'We might get lost. Perhaps we won't find the Only Elephant. It would be better to...'

But she couldn't think of anything it would be better to do. She was just putting off.

It was then that she realised she was on the edge of a wor, and at the beginning of a slippery slope which would carry her down to a moi and end in a very big boap, a deep muddy pool out of which she might never be able to struggle.

That couldn't happen. There was no going back. Often, at the end of all your thinking about whether or not to do something, you had to do it because you knew it was right, even though your thinking hadn't helped you to understand *why* it was right. So they went forward.

Twiga walked in a straight line, except when he had to go round trees that were not tall enough for him to go under.

A long time seemed to pass before Sheena recognised the clearing ahead of them, the one with the great screen of creepers that to begin with had hidden all of the Only Elephant except his enormous, gleaming eye.

There was no eye now. There was the same stillness, but no dark and massive shape behind the creepers, no elephant.

Twiga waited. Sheena sat. She found her thoughts drifting, because there was nothing else for them to do: she was at a loss.

'What's big and grey, has a trunk, and isn't there?'

'No elephants.'

The logic of that had puzzled Sheena when Thomas chortled it out on the drive North. A debate had started between Thomas and Dad Allen, about double negatives (Thomas had just started doing algebra at school). Surely if no elephants were not there, then some were? Or, alternatively, all of them were?

Thomas had tried the double negative trick on Amy (who hadn't understood the discussion) when they stopped for a picnic.

'You'd better tell me quick that you don't want me not to spread raspberry jam on Annie's face.'

Amy told him and spent the next half-hour crying and

cleaning Annie. When she had stopped crying she put jam in one of Thomas's shoes (he'd taken them off to paddle in a stream).

'Two wrongs don't make a right!' he'd complained when he found jam oozing between his toes.

'Ah, but maybe they can!' said his father. 'Isn't that another kind of double negative?'

The Only Elephant certainly wasn't there, that was the simple fact. There seemed little point in just going forwards. How about going sideways? Maybe a bit of lateral thinking would work here as well.

'We should stop looking for the Only Elephant, at least right now. We probably have more chance of finding the poachers. If we can get to where they'll enter the Forest we might be able to stop them, or slow them down.'

Twiga was very good at running, but not so good at thinking. He was happy to take orders from the Little General on his head. 'Alright,' was all he said.

Sheena thought she should leave a message of some sort in the clearing, for Mpole when he arrived; but how? The best she could do was jump down and scratch a simple drawing of an elephant in the dust in front of the screen of creepers, with its trunk pointing the way they would be going.

Twiga, once Sheena was back on his head, set off walking through the trees once more, ducking and bending when he had to, turning this way and that when necessary. He seemed to know which way was North. He walked until the trees began to get smaller and further apart. Before too long they were on the Forest's outskirts, then they were out of it altogether. Once clear of the trees Twiga could begin to gallop again, and he headed towards where he thought the track from Kinga Village lay. One problem, however, was that the muffled thumping of his hooves, which was loud even though the ground was soft, meant that they might not hear the pick-up if it was coming towards them. So every now and again Sheena told him to stop, so that they could listen.

They had halted for the fourth time. They were just about to set off again. There was a roar in the distance. Sheena knew it was the pick-up working hard on what was probably rough ground.

The Forest had thinned right out by now, and consisted only of acacia trees, set quite far apart. Through the trees she saw the track. They were coming to it at an angle. They would reach it before the pick-reached *them*. There would be time.

But for what?

Acacia trees. Thorn acacias. *Thorn* acacias. And what thorns! She remembered them well – long, hard and very sharp. Twiga knew all about acacias, and was expert at nibbling off their leaves without getting stabbed.

'Let's put thorn branches on the track!'

Twiga, once more, asked no questions. Sheena chose a part of the track next to a sharp curve. The surface of the track was smoother here, and the pick-up would be travelling more quickly when it reached the bend, even though it was at the top of a slight upwards slope. With luck the driver wouldn't see the thorns until it was too late.

The roar of the engine was closer. The thorn branches still growing on the trees were too tough to pull off, but there were lots of small branches lying on the ground. With Sheena's help Twiga selected a few, the ones with the biggest thorns. He picked them up carefully in his leathery mouth and laid them in a line across the track. There wasn't time to bury them.

'Snort on the track around them!' said Sheena. 'That will cover them with dust and make them less easy to see.'

Twiga's wide nostrils did a very good job. By the time the sound of the engine was close the thorns were well camouflaged.

Twiga and Sheena themselves were out of sight. Sheena had sent the giraffe off into the trees when he had finished, and she herself had crept into a shadow under a bush. She needed to learn as much as she could about the poachers and their plans.

With luck their plans would soon have to change.

The pick-up accelerated as it rounded the bend. All three men were in the cab. The driver probably didn't even see the thorns, but in any case there was no time for him to stop.

The pick-up didn't come to halt with a bang and a hiss, which is what Sheena had expected; but some of the thorns had obviously penetrated the tyres. Two branches spun with the wheels and rattled around in the wheel arches so that the driver could not fail to notice there was a problem. He braked sharply in a cloud of dust, and the pick-up stopped several yards beyond Sheena. The men got out and inspected the wheels. All four tyres had spikes embedded in them.

'Bad. That's bad. Too many thorns. All the wheels. Only one spare. Very bad.'

It had worked!

But the men began to work, too. They stripped off their ragged shirts (it was already hot) and set about dealing with the problem. They had all the equipment they needed, including good brains, and they thought their way through what needed to be done just as Mpole had thought his way through some of the Only Elephant's questions.

'Replace rear left with spare. Mend rear left. Replace rear right with rear left. Repair rear right,' and so on. Hakuna matata! No problem!

They brought out a scratched and battered foot pump, then a half-flattened tube of adhesive whose sharp smell made Sheena's nose wrinkle, even at that distance, as soon as they unscrewed the cap. For patches they cut up a piece of old inner tube.

Sheena was impressed. She noted how well they worked, and how well they worked together. And they were not angry, they were purposeful and almost cheerful. They seemed to be just normal, friendly men with a job to do.

As they worked and she watched Sheena had time to think some more...about double negatives, and about poachers. She decided that perhaps a double negative applied to the three men, too.

Yes, poaching was cruel and destructive and *mean*; and yes, elephants were in great danger of being killed off altogether, eventually; but the three men were obviously very poor. They probably had difficulty feeding their families, could not afford to take them to hospital when they were sick, might not be able to send their children to school. A great wrong had been done to them, and they were just trying to put it right, weren't they? Couldn't two wrongs make a sort of right, for them?

What a tangle! Even worse than that of the Forest she and Twiga had just struggled through!

She was beginning to get confused. But she knew that she had to keep her promise to Mpole. So she was also worried. She and Twiga had slowed the poachers down, but only by an hour or two. Not enough time for Mpole to get here with his trumpet.

She had crept closer to the pick-up while the men worked. They were busy at the front of the vehicle now, repairing the last tyre.

'Lucky. Just enough.'

They had squeezed the very last drop of adhesive out of the tube to mend the last puncture. The branches that the pick-up had *not* picked up were lying on the track a little way behind. Sheena crept back to them, staying out of sight. She nosed her way between the thorns on one of them, got her teeth around the branch itself, and lifted it carefully. Then she trotted quickly to the back of the pick-up and crept underneath it. As she went further in one of the thorns scratched the underside of the car, and she thought the men might have heard. But they carried on working.

She placed the branch carefully in front of one of the rear tyres, taking care that it didn't stick out where it would be seen.

That was all she had time for; but the pick-up was now booby-trapped. One more puncture, no more glue. She crept back to the bush and waited.

This time her device did not work. When the pick-up rolled forward the tyre just pressed the branch down into the loose dirt. The vehicle soon roared out of sight, leaving behind only a cloud of dust, a crushed thorn branch, and a disappointed cat.

Chapter Sixteen: Lisasi ya Tatu

Twiga ran as fast as he could, and even cut across most of the bends in the track, but could not catch the pick-up. Once or twice they heard its roar, no doubt as it struggled over a rocky patch or through sand, but when they next saw it, it was parked near a tree-fringed pool. The track stopped there. The pick-up was empty. The tarpaulins were still in the back, but the gun, axe and ropes had gone.

The pool was covered in bright green water-plants. Beyond it lay the darkness of the Dimdarong Forest. The poachers had set off into the trees in search of the Only Elephant.

'If only we could warn him. Maybe he's quite close. Is there any chance that you could make a sound like an elephant's rumble?' Sheena suggested. 'Or even trumpet a bit? A toot or two might do the trick.'

Twiga tried hard; but his attempt at a rumble came out as a mild burp, and his toot was no more than a breathy, wavering whistle. There was nothing else for it: they would have to follow the poachers into the darkness. Before they left Sheena scratched another elephant in the sandy earth.

There was something of a path to begin with, perhaps made by some of the few humans who had ever dared venture there. Soon, however, it became no more than a game trail, a faint track marking the occasional passage of animals. Then it petered out altogether and Twiga and Sheena had to guess which way to go.

'How do you find an Only Elephant in the forest?'

'Hide behind a tree and make a noise like the Only Banana.'

Sheena decided not to ask Twiga to attempt that.

The men ahead of them (if they were ahead, and not to one side, or even behind) were making no sound. The best Twiga could do was walk in a direct line away from the track: further into the Forest must be better.

To begin with he had difficulty keeping to a straight line. He could navigate easily over the great distances of the open plains, where everything was so visible. Among these thick trees, however, he soon began to lose his way. Sheena had to help; and it was like assisting Mpole with one of his thinking problems.

'Let's use where we've been to help us find where we're going,' she said. Twiga's height was a great advantage. He could look over the smaller trees, fix his gaze on a tall, distinctive tree ahead, walk to it, look back at the tall, distinctive tree they had left behind, then line up a further tree ahead of them, and so on.

When they set off the sun was well up in the sky. Before long, however, they could hardly see it: the Forest was too thick, the trees too overhead. Sheena was close to giving up.

'If we can't find the Only Elephant, maybe the poachers won't be able to either.'

But the poachers had found him. They had found him in another clearing, much further into the Forest than the one with the creepers. He was out in the open, not trying to hide. He stood looking straight at them as they emerged into the clearing. He was even bigger than they had been told. He was taller than some of the trees they had just stepped out from. They stopped, amazed. A gun could not kill such a beast.

A gun was all they had. So the man carrying it aimed it at the front of the elephant's great skull, just where his great brain would be.

That, then, was the scene as Twiga and Sheena also came out of the trees into the open space: the men standing together, fearful; the Only Elephant standing alone, calm; and the straight line connecting them and him, the line from the gun's barrel to his enormous forehead, the taut line along which the bullet would travel.

That was the scene into which Sheena jumped. Or, rather, jumped, ran and jumped again. Jumped down twenty feet from Twiga's head (and twisted and landed on her feet); ran across the hard ground towards the men; jumped, up this time, onto the barrel of the gun, just as the poacher pulled the trigger.

Her weight brought the end of the gun down, just as it went 'Bang!' The kick from the gun brought it up again, sharply, and threw her off; but not sharply enough to take it back on target. The bullet hit the ground in front of the Only Elephant. Earth flew into the air.

Sheena fell at the feet of another of the men. He lashed out at her with his worn shoes. His first kick missed, his second caught her painfully under the stomach and lifted her into the air and into a thick bush where she hung, drooping and breathless, like a piece of tired fruit.

The Only Elephant had not moved. Twiga had not moved. The man with the gun took aim again. Sheena was helpless. The second bullet would strike home.

Then, 'Barp!' in the distance. 'Barp! Barp!' It was the pick-up's horn. 'Bar-ar-arp!' It was the pick-up's horn being blown long and loud.

'No!' and 'Bang!' at the same time.

The 'Bang!' was the gun going off once more. The 'No!' came from the man who had kicked Sheena, the group's leader. As he cried out he stepped over to his companion and knocked the gun barrel upwards. The second bullet went up into the trees. A single leaf floated down into the brief silence.

'No! We cannot shoot the elephant now! That must be the Park Rangers, out on patrol. They have found our pick-up. They are telling us to return to it or they will come looking for us. If we hide the gun and go back we can tell them some story or other, and maybe pay them a little something. If we kill the elephant and they discover it we will have a big problem.'

'But they will have heard the gun!'

'We can say we heard it too, further off in the Forest. They may hold us while they look. But when they find nothing they will have to let us go.'

All of that made sense: the men might avoid trouble. More importantly, as far as Sheena was concerned, the Only Elephant would avoid being shot.

Then a terrible thing happened. It was terrible not just in itself, but because it need not *have* happened. That is what turns something which is already bad into a tragedy – the knowledge that it could easily have been avoided.

The Only Elephant stepped forward. He stepped forward slowly and heavily, lifted his massive trunk, and flapped his ears with a force that made the trees around him sway. He seemed to grow even taller as he did so, looming over the whole clearing and the men and animals in it.

One of the animals in it struggled to free herself from the bush into which she had been flung, as if she knew something dreadful was about to take place.

The man with the gun swung it up once more. He must have thought the Only Elephant was about to charge. Perhaps he was, perhaps he was. Just why he did what he did would remain as much of a mystery as the reason for his banishment from the herd so many years before.

The poacher, however, did what he did because he was terrified. He fired. The third bullet thudded loudly into the Only Elephant's broad chest.

Blood appeared, but not much blood. The real hurt was far inside.

The Only Elephant suddenly looked much older, if that was possible. His skin became even more wrinkled, as if it was now too big for him. His heavy tusks grounded. He fell on one knee. Then the rear leg on the same side collapsed under him and he began to keel over slowly like a great galleon which has hit an underwater rock, filled with water, and capsized.

The Only Elephant toppled sideways and fell with a crash that shook the whole of Dimdarong Forest.

A silence deeper than any Sheena had ever known settled over the clearing. More than an elephant had fallen.

Chapter Seventeen: Majina la Mwisho

The three men turned and scuttled away into the trees. They were probably going back to the pick-up to see if they were really in danger from the Park Ranger patrol. If not, they would return to remove the Only Elephant's tusks.

Twiga and Sheena arrived at the body at the same time, from opposite sides. There was no movement from the Only Elephant other than that of the small trickle of blood running down his chest. There was nothing they could do for him.

They set off back towards the pool where the poachers had left the pick-up. Sheena could not think of any better way of finding Mpole. She hoped he had realised what direction the poachers would be entering Dimdarong from, and had perhaps found the signs she had scratched in the dust. He needed to know what had happened.

They met him when they were half-way back to the pool. They heard him before they saw him. He had the gun in his trunk.

'What do you call an elephant with an AK47?'

'Sir.'

This AK47 was no longer a threat, however. Mpole was smashing it against a tree-trunk. In moments it looked more like a large pretzel than a weapon.

'I met the poachers running away. They are running away even faster, now. I heard them shooting. Is the Only Elephant safe?'

'No, he is not safe.'

Sheena did not want to say more.

'Take me there,' Mpole said.

The Only Elephant had not moved. The one eye they could see was open, but dull. He did not seem to be breathing. He seemed, to Sheena, to be dead.

'It takes a long time for an elephant to die,' said Mpole. He had walked around the great body slowly, in awe, and despair, and anger. There was something more adult in him than Sheena had seen before.

'For an elephant as old as the Only Elephant, it takes a very long time. He has begun a journey back into his past, and it is a very long past. When he gets to the time he was born, he will stop, for a moment. If he sets off again, and goes on beyond that, he will not come back.

We might be able to prevent him from going on, and *call* him back, if we used his First Name. If we could only bring him back, wake him up, and get him to stand, he might live. An elephant that lies down too long dies anyway, just because of the weight of his body. It crushes things inside him.

'But I don't know what his First Name is. Probably no elephant in the Baragandiri Herd knows what it is, now.'

'But isn't there any way of finding out?'

'We can look at him carefully. A First Name usually has to do with what makes an elephant different. Our First Name is important because it takes us back to the time when we were most special – the day we were born.

'When we are older we must be careful who we tell our first name to, since it is very powerful. I do not mind you knowing that my First Name was Twisted Tail: I trust you. My tail is straight now, however; and whatever gave the Only Elephant his First Name may not be true any more.'

Names that have power... Sheena remembered one of Amy's favourite fairy stories, about a dwarf with a secret name that could give people power over him. *Rumpelstiltskin*, that was it.

'Why don't we try something else before the Rumpelstiltskin Treatment? We could apply the Rumpledthickskin Cure – use a big thorn to prod him in his wrinkled rear end. That might wake him up.'

Her suggestion was only half-serious, and less than half-funny. She wanted to help, but felt helpless. That sometimes makes us say silly things. Mpole did not seem to have heard her, however.

'Look, look carefully,' he said. 'Find something special about him, something that will tell us what his First Name might have been.'

Sheena straight away decided that the fact that the Only Elephant was especially big would not count. She walked around the steep-sided island of his body, inspecting his enormous tusks (yes, there were two) and his great legs (four of those) and ears (two), tail (one). Eyes she would have to take on trust, since one was on the underside of his enormous head (one).

Mpole meanwhile was walking round in the opposite direction, looking increasingly agitated.

Sheena set off round the vast creature again. She would have to go into more detail this time.

The Only Elephant's feet were lying with their soles exposed. She counted the toenails on one of them. Six. Then she counted them on another. Six. The third had six also. No doubt the fourth would have the same number. Nothing odd there.

She was concentrating hard while she did that. She did not hear Mpole come up behind her. He too was looking very closely at the Only Elephant, and did not see Sheena. Twiga all the while had been standing looking down on the Only Elephant from his great height, hoping to see something special from above.

'Look out!' he cried.

Sheena jumped to one side just before Mpole set his foot down on her. She had very nearly begun the slow journey back into *her* past.

'What do you call a cat who's been stepped on by an elephant?'

'A large format doormat.'

'What do you call a computer mouse that's been stepped on by an elephant?'

'A three-and-a-half-inch floppy.'

'Watch where you're putting your great six-toed feet!' Sheena cried. She had had a lucky escape (what a mouse would have called a narrow squeak).

'What did you say?'

Mpole had swung round towards her.

'Six-toed? Elephants have only five toes.'

'The Only Elephant has six. Look! It's the same on every foot!' (She'd quickly checked the last one.)

'That's it! That must be it! Six Toes! That is his First Name!'

He knelt down next to the Only Elephant's head.

'Six Toes. Six Toes.'

He spoke softly. The Only Elephant did not move.

'Watch closely for any signs.' This time he was speaking both to Sheena and to Twiga, who had come up close.

Sheena jumped up onto Twiga's back, and then walked up his neck onto his head, from where she would have a better view. Twiga helped by stretching his neck out over the Only Elephant so that Sheena was looking directly down at the great head.

'Six Toes. Six Toes. Little Six Toes.' Mpole tried again.

Something was happening deep in the black pool of the Only Elephant's eye, something very strange. Sheena could see, down in its liquid darkness, the small shape of an elephant, walking towards her. It was the Only Elephant himself. She could tell it was him from the length of his tusks, even though the image itself was tiny. He was walking slowly, as if uphill, and he looked very tired. But he was coming closer all the time.

'He's coming back! I can see him coming back!' Sheena cried.

The Only Elephant in the Only Elephant's eye got bigger and bigger and clearer and clearer, and the eye itself got brighter and brighter. Then when there was nothing to see in there *but* elephant, and after that nothing but wrinkled skin, close-up, the walking elephant turned sideways. All that was visible now was his great eye, looking directly at Sheena and expanding all the while. The image of that eye continued to grow until it merged with the eye that held it, the Only Elephant's real eye. When the merging was complete the long eyelashes above the real eye flickered, the eye closed once, then it opened again and stayed open. The Only Elephant was back.

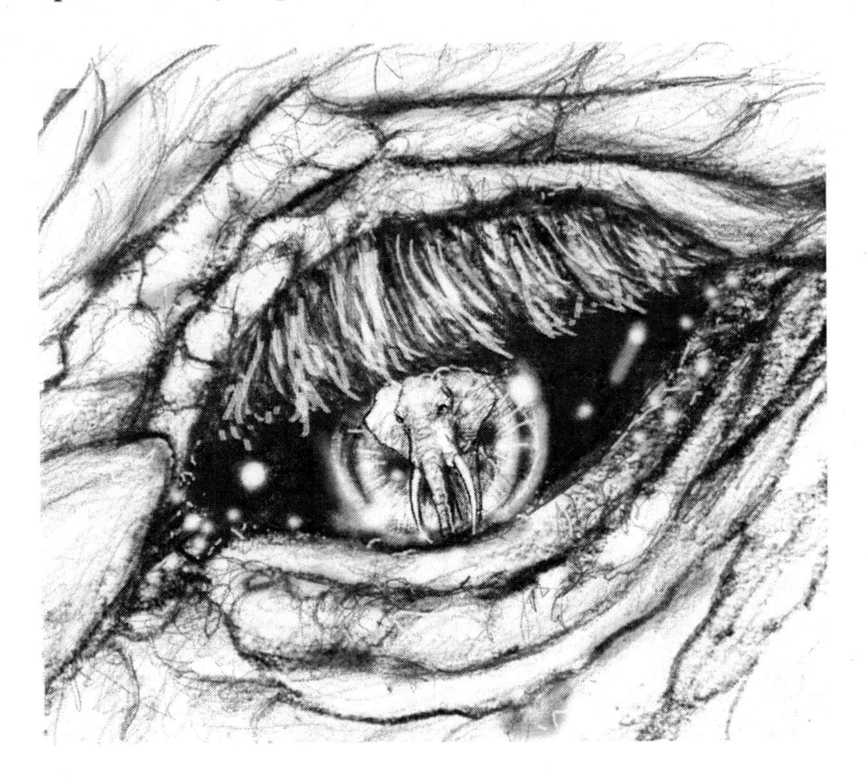

Chapter Eighteen: Adhimisho y Agano

'But he's got a bullet inside him. I saw it go in!'

Twiga and Mpole were struggling to get the Only Elephant onto his feet. They were pushing against his enormous, rounded shape from opposite sides. Twiga was leaning backwards against him, and had had to splay his legs out wide to give them greater pushing power and bring his bony rump low enough to get partly under the vast body. His legs were thin in relation to their length, but very strong. Mpole was pushing forward with his broad forehead, working it gradually under the Only Elephant's back half. The Only Elephant himself had made no movement.

It was Sheena who had spoken. She did not think it was a good idea to try and make the Only Elephant stand so soon.

'Don't worry about the bullet.'

The ground beneath them trembled with the words. They all jumped (even Mpole, which made the ground tremble even more). The Only Elephant had spoken, his great deep voice rumbling out as strong as ever.

'All animals have a bullet in them somewhere, something small deep inside, which one day will end their lives. I have had one since the day I was born. Now I have this other one; but it is not important, now. The first one will eventually kill me…but not today, not yet.

Sheena had heard Dad Allen talk to Mum Allen about a bullet with his name on it, once just before he went into hospital for an operation. Maybe that was what he had meant. Did she herself have one as well? Might it take away one of her nine lives?

She really ought to count up sometime to find out how many of those she had used up. Quite a few, since she started coming on safari and having adventures.

Encouraged by the sound of the Only Elephant's voice, Twiga and Mpole started leaning and heaving again. The Only Elephant himself helped by lifting his head and trying to push himself up. His legs and feet kicked massively as he did so, and Sheena, who had joined in by stretching up and giving the Only Elephant a little push of her own, had to jump a second time, quickly.

'Too many big feet around here!' she thought. But she was

pleased to see these four, each with its six toes, kicking so strongly.

It was not too long before the Only Elephant had his legs under him. Then, although they were dwarfed by him, Twiga and Mpole leant in again and pushed. With a great effort the Only Elephant straightened his knees...and he was standing once more, was once more as tall as some of the trees, was again, it seemed, as *strong* as a tree.

'Now you must walk,' said Mpole, speaking with both respect and authority.

'The herd is coming this way. They will want to see you. We can go to meet them.'

Mpole and Twiga stayed on either side of the Only Elephant. Sheena was back on Twiga's head. The Only Elephant walked slowly, but firmly. He said nothing about the presence of the little black-and-white cat, as if he had known all along that she would be there.

There were no other elephants in sight when they reached the pick-up. They stopped. The Only Elephant was unwilling to go any further from the heart of Forest.

Sheena was surprised to see the vehicle still standing where it had been left. Why had the poachers not taken it?

Then she saw that one of the rear tyres was flat. When she jumped down to look more closely she found a single thorn deeply embedded in the rubber. Her booby trap had worked after all, gradually.

But where were the Park Rangers? The ones who had blown the pick-up's horn?

'No Park Rangers. Only me,' said Mpole. 'I was going to blow my own horn to let you know I was coming. Then I thought some more about it and decided blowing the pick-up's would be better because it would make the poachers think they were in trouble.'

So he had pushed the centre of the steering wheel with the tip of his trunk, once, then twice more, then for a longer third time. The sound he made had saved the Only Elephant from the second bullet. It did not save him from the third.

'What happened when you met the poachers?'

'Nothing much. One of them pointed the gun at me, but when he tried to fire, it only made a clicking noise. When I charged him he threw it away and ran after the other two. I didn't chase them. I wanted to get to the Only Elephant quickly.'

Sheena was not altogether sorry that the poachers had escaped. Killing them would have been a third negative that would not have taken things any nearer to being back in balance. The Park Rangers would have had to hunt down the elephant that had done the killing (Mpole), and then there would have been more bullets.

She thought she had sorted out the double negative business, in fact. The truth was that a wrong act was *positively* bad, not negative at all. More wrong acts just added up, and suffering grew. So two wrongs *could* never make a right, and it was okay for Thomas to complain about the jam in his shoe.

It was not long before Sheena felt a shaking in the ground. The herd had arrived.

They arrived impressively, in large numbers, females and youngsters led by the Matriarch, large males following at a slight distance and off to one side. They were not running. The Only Elephant had done some rumbling while he waited with Mpole, Twiga and Sheena, and the herd seemed to know what they would find.

So the herd's mood when they got there was a strange mixture of calmness and excitement. They jostled around, greeting the Only Elephant, greeting Mpole, greeting each other even, as if they had not just travelled many miles together. There was much rubbing of shoulders, much intertwining of trunks, and some naughtiness among the baby elephants. This could only be described as a celebration. Twiga and Sheena wisely kept well out of the way.

Straight-Tusk was there, and some touching of trunks between her and Mpole went on as well, off to the side.

The celebration ended with a ritual. Somehow (Sheena didn't know how) it was decided that Mpole would stay in the Forest with the Only Elephant, for a while at least, in case the new bullet inside him began to do what bullets were made for. That was a great honour, it seemed. Mpole had become not only Accepted but Appreciated, and not just by the other young males, by the whole herd.

This was not a place for the herd to stay, and after a while Sheena could tell that they were preparing to leave. They left ritually. They left via the pick-up. No, that doesn't mean they piled aboard and left *in* it: they left *over* it.

The Matriarch was the first to step up onto the back of the vehicle. Its tail end went down suddenly and the front end lifted three feet in the air. She then stepped forward, the front end came down again with a crash, and the pick-up sagged in the middle. When she put her great forefeet onto the roof of the cab it sank under them into a pancake of crumpled, rusty metal.

Then the Matriarch stepped with great dignity down onto the bonnet, putting a great dent in it, and from there onto the ground. All the other elephants in turn walked up and over.

Those towards the end of the line didn't have to step up very far. By the time their turn came the tembolition was complete: the pick-up was belly-flat on the ground, its wheels splayed out sideways. The youngest elephants, who came last, walked over it with ease; and one particularly naughty one left something on the bonnet which symbolised the whole herd's anger and disgust at the use to which the vehicle had been put. It would take the dung beetles quite a while to find that and roll it away.

The herd set off North-East, at a steady pace. Sheena would need to go in the same direction, but much more quickly. Today was Saturday, and the Allens would leave the Park next morning. She needed to be safely tucked up, unseen, in the back of the Land Rover by then.

The Only Elephant turned and began to walk silently back into the Forest. Mpole also turned, and followed.

Sheena tried to think of something suitable to say to him by way of a farewell.

'Goodbye Mpole, and well done,' she said, but that was a bit ordinary. Then Mpole helped. He stopped walking and turned back towards her.

'Goodbye, little cat,' he said. 'Thank you. If you ever come back again and you want something done gradually…'

'*Stay* gradual,' Sheena said. 'Gradual gets there.' That was better.

She turned round on Twiga's head and looked backwards as he carried her off through the outskirts of the Forest. Mpole was standing still, looking after them. She watched as, against the darkness of the trees, he got smaller and smaller, gradually.

Chapter Nineteen: Kwaheri Tena

When they got to Tembo Campsite the Allens were gone. Plain gone.

Twiga had walked steadily through the night, not hurrying. Sheena had judged that they would reach the campsite well before the Allens had had breakfast and packed up. They were not early starters.

On this occasion they *had* started early. She found out as much from the vervet monkeys, who had wasted no time in invading the campsite to look for left-overs, or rather left-behinds. There were none, so the monkeys were rather disgruntled, and showed it in their loud chittering.

'Noisy people. Got up while it was still dark. Woke us up. Left just after sunrise. Took every last scrap with them. Nothing to eat here. May as well go somewhere else.'

Just after sunrise was maybe an hour earlier. Sheena was shocked and frightened. Awful thoughts started to flood in. She had been left behind. She might never get back home. She might never eat cat biscuits again, or walk over Thomas's homework, or put her nose in Amy's ear.

She could only hope that the family had not gone directly to the Park exit, but had set off for one last early-morning game drive on their way there. Just after sunrise, in fact, was the best time to see some of the animals before they hid themselves for the rest of the day.

'We need to go to the Park Gate as quickly as we can. They may still be there…or they may not be there yet.'

'Good riddance!' came a monkey voice from the tree above, as they set off. A custard apple just missed Sheena. Apparently vervet monkeys were not very good at remembering friends.

Finding the Land Rover was not so hard, after all. It was parked under a tree some way short of the Park Gate, with all four passenger doors open and the Allens standing a little way in front and off to one side. Dad Allen was behind the others, looking at a map. The door at the back of the Land Rover, however, was firmly shut.

So getting Sheena on board unnoticed was quite an involved process. It involved Twiga walking quietly towards the Land Rover from behind, with Sheena dangling from his tail. It involved the giraffe stepping carefully down the side of the vehicle and leaning slowly over Dad Allen's shoulder as if he too wanted to see the map. It involved the family making lots of loud noises like, 'Look out!' 'Wow!' 'Shoo!' and 'Annie – Stay out of sight!' It involved Sheena sliding down Twiga's tail while the family were making the loud noises, and sneaking through the long grass until she could jump up onto the rear seat and from there over into the back part of the Land Rover.

After the week's camping trip there was less in the Land Rover than there had been coming. The Allens had made a good job of eating their way through their rations, drinking their water, using up their spare diesel. Sheena made a good job of squirming her way down among the remaining boxes, bags and containers, and was soon completely out of sight. There was even room for her to turn around three times before settling down, to check that there were no sharp tent pegs in a position to insert themselves into the next few hours of her life.

Twiga, having made an equally good job of distracting the Allens, now ambled off into the trees as if what he had just done was perfectly normal. There had been no time for Sheena to say good-bye to him; but she had a feeling, this time, that she might be back.

Chapter Twenty: Bisha ya Mwisho ya Thomas

Thomas's Last Joke

'How did Tarzan address the elephant?'

'Me Tarzan. URLephant.'

The journey home seemed to take a long time.

There was a whole section in the middle, however, that Sheena knew nothing about.

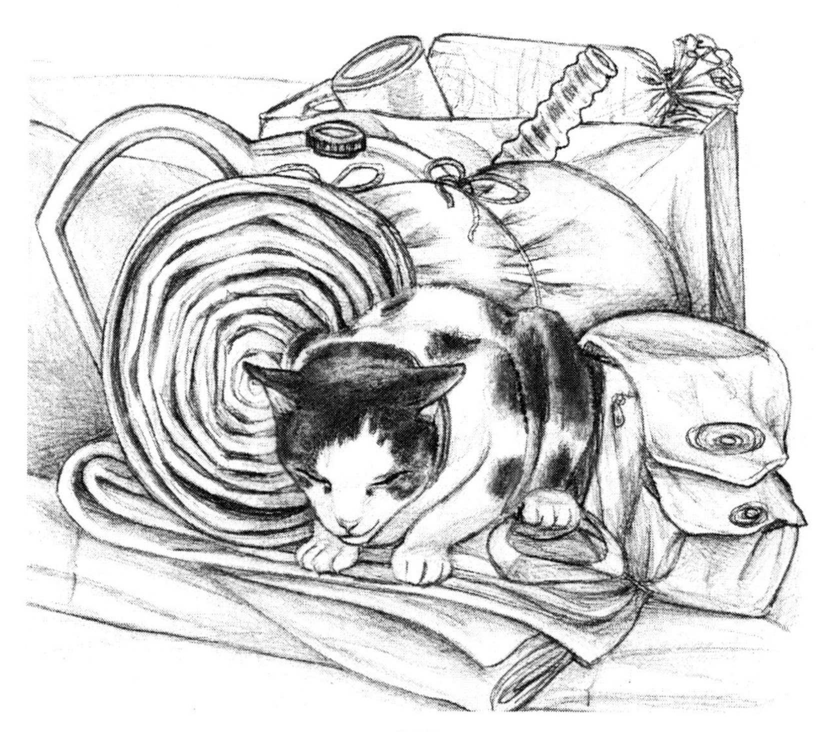

'..but she had a feeling, this time, that she might be back' (Page 214).

The phrase, 'this time' is a reminder that Sheena has been to Baragandiri before. You may have read about the adventures she had then, in *Paka Mdogo.* If not, imagine the map on Pages 6-7 covered, not with Mpole icons, but with those of a mysterious bird, and with many Sheena pawprints. That will give you some idea of how far she travelled on that first occasion, in order to find Thomas and Amy and save them from an old and terrible lion.

Then there's the arrow in the top left-hand corner of the map, pointing to The Dry Highlands. That's where *The Meerkat Wars* take place. It's a very different part of Baragandiri, and the challenges Sheena faces there are also very different – and they're greater, and more important, than any she's faced in the Park so far...